Mollie Hardwick is the author of many historical novels, most recently *The Merrymaid* and *Girl with a Crystal Dove*. She is also known to television viewers as the author of *Upstairs Downstairs*, *By the Sword Divided* and the *Juliet Bravo* series. However, she has had a lifelong interest in detective fiction, which was responsible for her knowing Dorothy L. Sayers, to whom this book is dedicated. With her husband Michael Hardwick, she has written many books and plays incorporating Sherlock Holmes.

The Hardwicks live in a fifteenth-century house in Kent, which is also home to two cats, Hudson and Marigold.

D0465481

Also by Mollie Hardwick

MALICE DOMESTIC
PARSON'S PLEASURE
UNEASEFUL DEATH
THE BANDERSNATCH
PERISH IN JULY

and published by Corgi Books

THE DREAMING DAMOZEL

Mollie Hardwick

CORGI BOOKS

THE DREAMING DAMOZEL

A CORGI BOOK   0 552 13665 4

Originally published in Great Britain by Century
a division of the Random Century Group

PRINTING HISTORY
Century edition published 1990
Corgi edition published 1991

This book is set in 10/12pt Plantin
by Kestrel Data, Exeter

Corgi Books are published by Transworld Publishers Ltd,
61-63 Uxbridge Road, Ealing, London W5 5SA, in Australia by
Transworld Publishers (Australia) Pty Ltd, 15-23 Helles Avenue,
Moorebank, NSW 2170, and in New Zealand by Transworld
Publishers (NZ) Ltd, Cnr Moselle and Waipareira Avenues,
Henderson, Auckland.

Printed in Great Britain by
BPCC Hazell Books
Aylesbury, Bucks, England
Member of BPCC Ltd.

CHAPTER ONE

The longcase clock looked down at Doran with, she fancied, a melancholy expression on its brass face.

Understandably. One of the delicately wrought iron hands was broken off at the shaft. The dial, which should have shone like a miniature sun, was dull with scratch marks and what appeared to be small lumps of some brownish foodstuff, as though the person who had applied brass polish to it too enthusiastically had at the same time been eating spaghetti Bolognese. The spandrels, pretty decorative scrolls at each corner, had been crudely overpainted in bright gilt.

The case, so gracefully made, had suffered equally. Doran Chelmarsh, stripping patiently away at the wood, had now reached the eighth coat of paint, in colours ranging from damson to poison green. Miraculously, the wood's surface had survived undamaged and was emerging palely. But the door to the heavy lead weight and the pendulum had been replaced with a modern one on mass-produced hinges. There were holes in the bottom of the case which might have been made by rats.

Doran moved away, out of the fumes of stripping fluid. She pulled off her heavy gloves and sat down to contemplate her work. On the whole, the poor maltreated clock gave her pride, satisfaction, pleasure. She could do a lot of the restoration work herself. The professional she employed would do the rest – at a price. At least she knew the worst now: the people who had mishandled the clock over two and a half centuries had somehow not destroyed the work of a humble Hampshire maker, John Hobson, whose engraved name she had exposed on the lower half of the dial. Howell would be pleased.

Howell Evans. Her friend and, until a few months ago, colleague and partner of Fairweather Antiques, the shop in the old harbour quarter of Eastgate. The town was quietening down after the seaside tourist season. It was September, and the air was already bringing ashore some of the English Channel's chill. The day visitors had beaten their retreat – the rubberneckers who wandered in, priced objects, picked up delicate pieces and set them clumsily down again, and went out having bought none, or the smallest, cheapest of them they could find.

Years of experience had given Doran a sixth sense that could detect those who meditated leaving with goods slipped into handbag or pocket. She had developed a way of asking 'Would you mind putting that back?' that gave no offence, while her smile even suggested a degree of complicity. In her early thirties, her beauty still had its Botticellian quality: the longish face, delicate features and large bright eyes, the stem-like neck, the soft brown curls of hair clinging to her neck as the curls of cherubs do in antique art.

Or so Rodney said, after years of marriage to her. He had never ceased to wonder at his luck in winning Doran; a luck mirrored in the eyes of the other men as they took in, among her other attributes, his wife's slender figure and elegant, long, perfect legs.

Only Howell stayed unmoved by such things. Howell wasn't a ladies' man, never had been. Quite the opposite, she knew from his relationships, though nowadays, so far as Doran knew, he was living alone in his Eastgate cottage. He seemed to be drinking less than in earlier days, and smoking fewer of the noxious cigarettes which made all around him cough painfully. But the Welshness was still there, the sharp eye for a bargain and for quality. He hadn't lost that something in his manner that Doran thought of as a dark smoulder.

His decision to break their partnership hadn't been easy, he'd told her, and she knew he meant it.

'I wouldn't chuck you for just any job, you know that, *merch*. But it's Bartleby Galleries, and the pay's terrific. Keep me in my old age, it will, if I start stashing some away.'

'Don't you mean your middle age? These days they don't shoot you at fifty, do they?'

Howell shrugged. 'Got to grab at chances.' He looked round the small shop, its quality stock sadly reduced and getting harder to replace. 'Not much left in this for me, is there?'

'Not a lot for me, either, without you. You've always been the financial side of it. How am I going to manage?'

'You'll make out, gal. Tell you what, I know this accountant guy up in town – handles some stuff for me, insurance and that. He'll sort the figures out for you.'

'Thanks. Just what I need, someone extra to pay. What are you insured against, anyway – twins, shipwreck, spontaneous combustion? Sorry, Howell,' she added quickly. She knew how easily his emotions welled up. He'd been trying not to cry. Her waspishness had helped him.

'I'm sorry too, Doran. Not doing it for fun. Only, I've got to, see? Offer I can't refuse. Look, can't you pack the shop in? Live off your old man?'

Doran was able to laugh at the picture this raised in her mind.

'Rodney's not exactly the traditional steady wage-earning husband, you know. Rebel vicar, with one service a month at a village church. A talk spot on local radio – at least that's once a week – and his Local Lore piece in the county newspaper. Not what might be called af-fluence. Anyway, I wouldn't want to live off him. And I love all this.'

She caressed the surface of a charming Caughley jug; it had only the tiniest piece missing from its rim. Knowing her vulnerability, Howell felt even more like a monster. But sentiment couldn't outweigh the salary Bartleby's had offered. His share of the little shop's takings came nowhere near. He patted Doran's hand, his nearest approach to physical tenderness.

'I'll be around if you want me. Just give me a bell. Or put a chit through the cottage door. Any trouble, hassle, somebody tryin' to do you down . . . you know.'

'I know.' The smile was back in her eyes. 'And I'm sorry I didn't just say I understand. I do. And I wish you lots, lots of luck.'

Scrubbing at the clock again, she reflected that she was doing this hard messy work for Howell, in a way, though he would get none of the profit she hoped to make from it. He was a clock man, with a special passion and knowledge which Doran knew she could never equal. Crown wheels, check-springs, winding pinions, strike flirts, detents, cams: she had never come to terms with them – some divergence of the female mind from the male, maybe. Or was that a sexist thought? Perhaps there were supremely talented, natural-born female clock-makers and horologists, unknown to her.

But at least she had taught her six-year-old son to tell the time. She smiled at the thought of Kit, serious-minded like his father, yet with the same streak of eccentric humour. He would be home from school when she got back, important with the doings of the day, hungry for Vi Small's food. Vi was so sensible about not forcing a child to eat when it didn't want, and adding an exotic grown-up touch now and then to tempt the youthful appetite.

If only Vi cost less. Now that she had let her other jobs around the village of Abbotsbourne go, so that she could work at Bell House full time, her wages made a considerable hole in Doran's profits which, since Howell had gone, were very slender – too slender for security.

It seemed, on the face of things, silly to spend so much time at the shop and about its affairs, when she could have been at home and looking after Kit and the house herself. Some other dealers in Eastgate had taken to spending only a routine day or two at their shops, confining their buying to local auctions and fairs. Doran could see this coming for herself, if not something more drastic. But then, to give up the excitement of the perpetual treasure hunt for the rare and lovely object just around the corner, the piece in poor condition which only she would recognize for what it was: how could she relinquish that?

And she must, out of pride, contribute something to the family income. Rodney was lucky to have a church at all, even for one Sunday a month, where he could hold the Authorized Version services he loved; and even if, as he hoped, he was alloted another, twenty miles away, it wouldn't mean double the pay or even a petrol allowance. The authorities considered him a dangerous reactionary, not to be encouraged.

If only Jim Fontenoy, manager of Radio Dela, would give him a staff job as well as his little weekly talk on this or that curiosity in the station's catchment area. With his beautiful speaking voice he could be a splendid announcer. Or a cricket commentator. But, of course, there'd be queues of eager young men and women, with or without beautiful voices, in line for any such vacancies.

No, she must keep the shop going somehow. To stay

away from it would be to miss what little trade there was; to stop going out buying would mean she'd have no stock. Stalemate.

She had not meant to let the shop worries spill over into home life. But it was hard not to confide in Rodney.

Doran surveyed him fondly. Forty-five plus, the curling, untidy hair more grey than brown now, the ascetic face more lined, the down-droop of the eyelids at their outer corners betraying middle age as much as myopia. Yet to Doran that serene scholar's face was as attractive as it had been when their marrying had seemed impossible. Beauty lives with kindness. Who said that? Rodney would know; he knew where all such things came from.

' "Beauty lives with kindness"?' Not even a crease of thought or momentary puzzlement on the high, line-etched brow which matched the brain behind it. The heavy-rimmed spectacles glinted benevolently. 'Two Gents. *Two Gentlemen of Verona*, to term them more tastefully. It's the song "Who is Sylvia?" Proteus is two-timing Julia, you remember, so he sends musicians to serenade . . .'

'Yes, yes,' Doran said hastily, cutting off a dissertation. 'It doesn't matter about the plot. Just something that crossed my mind.'

'I thought you looked distrait when you came in. Are you distrait, my darling?' Rodney laid down his fork, prepared to listen.

'Not unbearably. Only money, as usual. There isn't a lot coming in from the shop account, and so many people seem to be holding out their hot little hands for it when it does come.'

Rodney shook his head. 'If only you needn't work. If only Radio Dela paid me more . . . Look, shall I go and address them? Tell them my wife has to work in a sweatshop from dawn to dusk – "stitch, stitch, stitch, in poverty, hunger and dirt, a woman sat in unwomanly rags . . . " '

'They'd be deeply moved, but I doubt to the extent of raising your pay. No, that's not the answer. What I thought, while I was paint-stripping this afternoon . . .'

The door opened. 'Kit's come to say good night,' announced Vi.

Beside her upright, tall figure, Kit appeared an elfin child from one of the fairy pictures that decorated the nursery. He had inherited the fine bone structure of both parents, and features which were a subtle blend of theirs. His hair, damp from the bath, sprang in dark tendrils. He was a great deal tougher than he looked.

'Can I have one of your church books in bed, Daddy?' His voice was clear and precise, so far untouched by the local twang that prevailed in the village school.

Rodney was on his feet, halfway to the bookshelves. 'Which one tonight?'

Kit pondered, head on one side.

Doran objected, 'He sits up so long looking at the pictures.'

'It's all right, Mummy. It helps with reading, and I'll go to sleep soon.'

'He will, you know,' Vi confirmed with pride. 'He's very good and he knows ever such a lot of words from his Daddy's books.'

It was true, though they were mainly words not in daily domestic use, such as apse and sedilia, helm and effigy. Kit liked the sound of words, whether or not he fully realized their meaning. His parents were unworried about his addiction to Rodney's collection of church guides, dating from the happy days of the 1930s and showing ancient, lovely buildings, not yet ravaged by Hitler or the Devil's other agents, developers. Later, Kit might be taken over by computer games, but at least he would know what books were.

They kissed him, and he them, with a warm talcum-scented hug. Rodney watched him out of the room wistfully. Doran, as she always did at Kit's bedtime, thought of the second child she had carried for only three months, the previous year. They had wanted it so much, but her body had rejected it, to their bitter disappointment. Since then there had been no promise of another, only hope, regularly kindled and regularly dashed. Perhaps, if Doran could stop driving to and from Eastgate, and to and from auctions and the stockrooms of other dealers, and worrying about profit margins, there would be a peaceful time when she could rest and gather her physical and mental forces.

Rodney read her mind, as he so often did, and brought her back to the point Kit's entry had checked.

'You were saying? Paint-stripping . . . ?'

'Oh, yes. I always think of other things when I'm doing it, it's so boring. What I need is a specialist line – something I *like* buying and selling; something I know about.'

'You know about so much.'

'Yes, but too many things – fans, and porcelain and pottery, and pictures. If you handle too many lines people don't really rate you, like they do Howell for his clocks.'

Rodney nodded. 'As in the theatre. When an actor's too versatile they don't let him play Hamlet. Look at Irving . . .'

'Love to, but I need to think hard about this. All dealers have got something they know about specially. What would you say was mine?'

'Well. Figurines? Little pottery people? Queen Victoria. Politicians. Murderers. Sheep leaning up against blossom-trees.' His eyes roved for further inspiration along their well-filled dining-room mantelpiece.

'Called bocage, actually.'

'Like the greenery one's supposed to put in Pimm's?'

'That's borage. The trouble is, the small-collectables market's shrinking. The shop dealers are getting knocked out of it by the fairs. Antiques fairs, boot fairs, where people who would never come into a shop can pick up something they fancy, and sell something they're tired of or think might be worth a bit. The jug they're sure is Clarice Cliff, for its jazzy blue and yellows. Anyway, they go home happy.'

'Innocent merriment.'

'Maybe. But what they don't know is that they're buying from dealers trading on the cheap, from hired stalls with no overheads. And what they're selling to the public has been picked over by the other dealers first. So the prices are trade prices, only a bit lower because you don't need such a big profit margin if you're not running an expensive shop.'

'There's your answer, then,' Rodney said with jokey reassurance. But he understood. He had understood for a long time that Doran was fighting a losing battle with her chosen profession. For her sake, he tried to retreat from that knowledge. These days it seemed to him that he was mentally retreating from more and more threats to their peace and comfort. He supposed that was why he took refuge so readily in flippancy and academic side issues.

'Yes,' he said. 'I know it's tough. Not the old image of the dealer surrounded by objects of art and of virtue, graciously agreeing to sell one occasionally.' Their own home, he was aware, had lost a good many of their fine pieces of furniture that Doran had rescued from stock and brought back for them to live with. Like pet sheep in a thin season, they had been returned to market.

He had known, but had chosen not to comment.

'I used to like my figurines,' Doran said wistfully. 'Everything from cheap and cheerful to wonderful Derby. Now, I'd even be grateful to find a bust of John Wesley.'

'Wesley – curious man.' Rodney was off. 'Did you know he founded his very own religious society in Savannah? The Americans took to him like anything at first, then started going off him because he bossed people around so heavily. Then' – Rodney was warming to his subject – 'he went too far by denying a lady Communion after she'd rejected his proposal of marriage, so he gave up trying and came back to England. Imagine Wesley in Savannah – the defence of the Salwanners – where John Willet lost his arm, you know . . .'

Doran made, with difficulty, the connection between Rodney's rambling remarks and *Barnaby Rudge*.

'Yes, very odd,' she said kindly. 'But about specializing . . .'

Rodney was momentarily disappointed. He would have enjoyed telling her about Wesley buying a disused gunfoundry and making it into a chapel. He concentrated his mind on what she was saying. 'Not pottery, then?'

'Not. So much of it's faked. Fakers can age modern pieces so easily. Give them false marks, craquelure, all sorts of tricks. I always know, or think I do, but there could be a time when I really didn't. Anyway, pottery's not unusual enough.'

'Oh.' Rodney's gaze wandered to the desk by the window, and the pile of books he would fillet to make up his next Local Lore column. Antique objects were not, strictly speaking, his subject. He struggled to think of something useful that was.

'Manuscripts? No, I suppose not. Pictures?'

'Mm. I've done well with pictures, on the whole. But

14

they're getting terribly scarce, the worthwhile ones, like everything else. When it comes to selling repros of old advertisements as decorations, I give up – I wouldn't have them in the kitchen.' Doran's kitchen was, in fact, a small museum of treasures living amicably with modern technology.

'Small boy in bath, crying for bar of soap,' Rodney recalled. ' "He won't be happy till he gets it." Tramp with filthy face – "Ten years ago I used your soap and since then I have used no other." Odd how the soap ones come to mind.'

'I don't think the tramp would have much pictorial appeal,' Doran reflected. 'The small boy might. Big dogs, little girls, buxom milkmaids, small boys, yes. Tramps, no. Well, pictures are a thought, all the same. I'll just have to work it out. It would mean going further afield, oh dear. Why are you looking so remote?'

Rodney focused his eyes. 'Was I? I was only wondering why I included murderers when I was suggesting pottery subjects. We haven't any figurines of murderers, have we? I hope not.'

'We haven't, ourselves. But there was a whole range of Victorian murderers made for people to buy who didn't get newspapers and couldn't read in any case. They got told about them, and bought the figures to stand on the mantelpiece. James Rush shooting Isaac Jermy. William Corder killing Maria Marten in the Red Barn – he knifed, shot, and strangled her, a very thorough man.'

'Which did the figure show him doing?'

'All three. Separate figures. And, of course, there was Palmer the Poisoner. I only wish I had some to sell. They fetch a lot now.'

'Curious,' said Rodney, 'how popular crime's always been. No, it isn't curious. Sin always has to have its alluring side, or the Devil would be out of business and I'd be out of work, so far as the Church goes.'

Both of them thought of the real-life murders in which they had innocently become involved in the past. The psychological sadist, the killer for antique loot, the person who murdered for love and reprisal. The kidnapper with one particular shining reward in mind: that crime had touched them the most personally. And the crime that was freshest in their minds, the bloody end of one who perished one hot night in July before the breaking of the storm.

'I hope we shan't come across any more,' Doran said. 'Though they came across us, to be accurate, didn't they?'

' "I met Murder on the way – he had a mask like Castlereagh." ' Rodney was apt to be visited by other men's muses at any time of the day or night. He was unable to resist ending the verse:

' "Very smooth he looked, yet grim; seven blood-hounds followed him." Does that remind you of anybody?'

'Yes. Do you want more pie?'

Rodney looked into the deep pie-dish, where the blackberries glistened darkly under the jagged overhang of creamy pastry, as though a sheet had been turned roughly back to reveal something.

'Thanks, no,' he replied.

The evening was a good time for strolling. The sun was down now, the red-gold streaks of its setting slowly fading among banks of dark cloud, like embers dying behind the bars of a grate. A strange light, this autumn dusk, thought Doran, walking alone: 'Light thickens, and the crow makes wing for the rocky wood.'

Curious, how the unlucky Scottish Play haunted one at this hour, even in the quiet streets of Abbotsbourne.

It was not a favourite of hers; unpleasant in content, and near-impossible to stage convincingly. Murder for gain, and black witchcraft. Rodney, speaking for the Church, had said that witches did indeed exist, and presented a serious problem when they misused their powers.

'I don't know about the ones who cook with herbs, and undress to dance by the light of the moon, but I suspect them of mixed motives.'

'Remember Stella Meeson?' she had reminded him.

'Who could forget? Praying naked to Ashtaroth in the cricket pavilion. I'd warned her not to meddle with such things. Spoken to her sharply, but it made no more impression than – well, than one's average sermon makes on one's average congregation.'

'Stella was more than slightly dotty. But you believe there are true witches?'

'And warlocks.' She remembered that Rodney had touched the little gold cross he always wore. 'People who play with fire – potential hell-fire.'

A tree branch over Doran's head shed a flurry of dead leaves in a sudden gust of wind. She shivered, then rebuked herself for silly nervousness. Her nerves had been unusually sensitive just lately, she knew. Too much time alone in the shop? Too much brooding, worrying?

Her walk had taken her beyond Mays Lane, where her own Bell House stood, a pretty road of old houses, cottages and gardens, already beginning to be in-filled with new dwellings that were slowly settling into the landscape. It was easy to despise neo-Queen Anne when one lived in genuine Queen Anne; but that too had been new once. And there was no doubt that Abbotsbourne was changing, from a quiet grey valley-village in a fold of the beautiful North Downs to a link in the chain of places that brought England and France closer, with more and more traffic grinding and roaring through it.

The shops in the little square were changing, too. Old shopkeepers had retired or moved away, exiled by increased rent and rates. Jack Turner the butcher was still there, helped in the shop now by his silent, gangling son Arnold. The greengrocer-florist who let the church buy flowers on such easy terms was still there, as he deserved to be, and the mini-market run by smiling Asians, that had once been an old-fashioned grocer's. The pretentious boutique had gone. Yet another estate agent had arrived to rival the established Dixter and Wylie's, where, whatever the state of the market, lecherous Rupert no doubt continued to make enormous sums of money – and a corresponding number of women. Something remained constant, even if only Rupert.

At the corner of the square the spire of St Crispin's Church pointed at the darkening sky. Rodney had been its vicar when he and Doran first met, and marriage between them couldn't have seemed more unlikely. The cleric who had taken his place, Edwin Dutton, still ruled the parish with an inflexible grip in no way related to his limp handshake. Now the south aisle housed machines for coffee and tea, and gravestones there were covered with heavy-duty carpet. The cushions stacked in a heap in the vestry were for sitting on, in and out of service time, by the younger members of the congregation, and those of the not-so-young who believed that social integration mattered more than aching muscles and creaking joints, as they listened to gospel songs and guitars.

The wonderful reredos of carved alabaster was no longer behind the altar of the Lady Chapel. By order of the Reverend Edwin, with very reluctant parish support, it had been taken to pieces and stored in a bank vault, together with the church silver, a seventeenth-century chalice and two dish patens. They might very well be sold at some time for the benefit of the church and of the

Reverend Edwin's pet charities, if silly people would stop murmuring about wanting them back in place.

The vicar's tight mirthless smile seemed for a moment to illuminate the dark churchyard, the leaning headstones and ivied table-tombs. Doran saw him as one of those medieval tomb-figures of Death.

She walked round the church, coming out by the small gate that led to Cow Lane, above the High Street. She had left home intending to walk to the ruins of the castle up on the hillside, to look down at the village lights as she often did in the evening stillness. But the wind suddenly struck chill, even through her warm coat. She turned and walked swiftly back, over the familiar ground to the most familiar place of all. Home.

Rodney had forgotten to draw the curtains. He was still at his desk, note-making, wholly absorbed. The lamplight picked out silver gleams in his hair. As she watched he took off his spectacles and smoothed a hand over tired eyes. It was a gesture that especially meant Rodney to Doran, and sent a surge of love through her.

Moonlight was shining on Kit's bed when she went up later to look into his room. Vi had left the curtains open so that he could see the sky. The room was still a nursery. His Lewis Carroll figures were still displayed under their glass case, but Kit seldom looked at them now, and never played with them: the room had undergone a subtle transformation into something belonging to a boy. Doran sometimes wondered whether the little grotesque companions of Alice were not a self-indulgence of her own. It would be hard to part with them ever, unthinkable to trade them in for profit, which was the obvious thing to do just now.

The moon slid abruptly behind clouds, leaving the form of the sleeping Kit a motionless shape under the bedcover knitted by some past lady of Doran's family. Very softly she shut the door and went downstairs to Rodney and the living-room fire.

Even there, kneeling on the rug, she couldn't repress another shiver. Rodney turned away from the television screen, on which an earnest, bearded figure was demonstrating some excavations.

'Got a chill?'

'No, I don't think so. It was just . . . a silly feeling.'

'Not a premonition – I hope?'

'I don't have them. You're the one who does, remember? I was walking round the church. A sort of feeling of – it's hard to describe – of evil came over me. It's gone now.'

'Was it to do with us – you, or me, or Kit?' Rodney took matters of the soul very seriously.

'I don't think so.' She leaned against his knees. 'After all, walking in a churchyard at dusk isn't conducive to merriment, is it? A train of rather morbid thought, I'd say. Let's forget it. Don't you think we ought to change Kit's room round a bit? I thought it looked rather babyish just now.'

'What had you in mind? Cricket bats, sporting rifles, sweatshirts with soccer logos?'

'Horrible! But some of the decor may have been there too long. There might be pictures he'd like better than – well, Dürer's *Hare*. I can't see it any more, I take it for granted, and it's only a modern print. Why don't I ask Kit how he feels, and whether he'd mind if we scrapped it?'

'I think, my darling, you'd find that he'd mind very much about losing something he's known all his life. Children are seriously conservative. At that age, they need the familiar. He won't let me change the words ever so slightly in a bedtime story.'

20

Doran remembered that the picture had belonged to Rodney's first child, Helena, Kit's crippled half-sister, who had died some years ago. She agreed hastily, 'Same with me. I've tried skipping bits, but he won't have it. Oh, well, I'll leave the Dürer. You know what it is? I feel like buying pictures – that's all.'

Howell tossed the leaflet on to Doran's lap. They had met at the Port Arms, Eastgate's harbour pub, frequented by the town's remaining antique dealers; a dark, stuffy, highly camped-up tavern with a great many artificial black-painted beams. It was their first meeting since Howell had started his London job.

'I don't believe it,' she said. 'Stargate Manor, at the other end of our valley? I've never heard of it, and I don't miss many country sales. Why's it being sold up? Who's the owner?'

'Old chap died. Executors' sale. Catalogue's not a thrill a line, but I thought I'd look in, inspect some of those bureaux and what they're calling Old Mantelshelf Clocks. Funny language these locals use. Don't know many words, do they? Still, you never know. Might be all rubbish, or there might be a Knibb or two. Listen to me give a hollow laugh.' He demonstrated.

Doran was reading the auction catalogue. ' "Quantity of beds, twelve dining chairs, bookcases, kitchen and garden furniture . . ." Not many Knibbs or Vulliamys likely to turn up in that lot. I've been to so many sales of tacky tat, and I can't afford to lay out money on it any more. How did you come by this? Isn't it a bit beneath your new status?'

'It was at the cottage. Lying on the floor amongst the bills. Viewing tomorrow, ten. You'll come, won't you? Breath of fresh air.' He inhaled deeply of the Port Arms' smoky, beery fug.

Doran hesitated, scanning the list of lots. ' "China swan. Imari bowl. Quantity of chamber pots." I don'think . . .' She turned the page, and her attention was captured.

'Pictures. Street Scene, Italy. Highland Landscape. Nude girl on beach. Fiesta Day, Madrid. Man with child – well, that makes a change. Young woman in costume. Sheep grasing. Head of Edwardian Lady.' She folded the catalogue decisively. 'There might be something interesting. Woolly descriptions, but perhaps they don't know themselves. Right, I'll come.'

Howell accompanied her back to the shop to view her progress with the longcase. An admiring whistle greeted him from Doran's dealer neighbour, Meg Rye, for once without her artist husband, Peg.

'Nice, Howell, nice. Given up the jeans, have we?'

He smirked. His short, squarish figure was still uneasy in the dark blue town suit he was practising wearing. His usual clothing would have melted into the background on a building site.

'Got to dress up to the job, haven't I? Can't patronize you all the time, Meg.' Meg sold secondhand clothes.

Doran unlocked her shop door. There was post on the floor. Circulars, invoices, and something familiar – another catalogue of the Stargate Manor sale.

'Well, they certainly mean all the local trade to know about it. Perhaps they're not so woolly, after all. Very enterprising of Messrs Clegg and New. Almost Tegg and Ewe. Come to think of it, they do sell sheep as well. How appropriate.'

The salerooms were on the outskirts of an undistinguished village to the north-west of Abbotsbourne and the cathedral town of Barminster. The countryside changed as they drove out of the wooded valley and

ounded chalk downs, becoming flat and pedestrian, with
motorway and many bright-bricked 'executive' houses,
clones of some developer's architect's vision of Tudor
with a touch of Plantagenet and double garage. Doran
was driving them, in her now-venerable estate car. She
switched on the wipers as thin rain began.

'Pity they aren't selling from the house,' she remarked.
'Stargate. Lovely, romantic name. A doorway into the
constellations . . .'

'Hang on to your dreams,' Howell said. 'It's the worst
kind of Victorian, in the middle of a housing estate. Land
sold off long ago.'

The saleroom was a hangar-like building that Doran
had been to a few times before. She had never come
away with anything exceptional. They hurried across the
sparsely occupied car park, in steady cold rain.

'Funny how it always rains, out in the sticks,' Howell
grumbled.

'You're spoilt, up in Mayfair. I bet you take taxis
everywhere.'

'Matter of fact, I do. Got to treat good clothes proper.'
He was in no danger of spoiling them this morning, back
in his old Eastgate working gear, a battered and faded
denim outfit with some of the poppers missing. Good
enough for a viewing day.

There were not many people inside, mostly curious
locals. Doran didn't recognize any of the few who were
obviously dealers.

'It's a "We Buy Anything" day,' she said. 'From the
look of this junk, they're welcome to it.'

A more leisurely stroll round revealed nothing to
redeem the dull-faced ranks of furniture, mostly of
twentieth-century making: chairs upholstered in leather-
ette, kitchen pine, chain-store reproduction a long way
after the originals, sad bed frames, a small snooker table

23

with torn baize and pockets that the balls would have gone straight through. Deflated curtains in unpopular colours, worn carpets that had never been further East than the exotic East Riding of Yorkshire.

'Poor things.' Doran touched the flattened pile of a rug. 'Nobody loved them, and now nobody will, unless it's couples starting up home on cheap secondhand. Oh dear.'

'You're too soft.' Howell was examining contemptuously what the catalogue had termed Old Mantelpiece Clock. It was 1950s, probably not even in working order. He didn't trouble to investigate. Its companion on a clumsy Victorian sideboard was a miniature clock of probable Swiss origin, its china body decorated with transfers of flowers and a Venus attended by Cupid.

'At least it's decorative,' Doran remarked. 'You could do it up.'

Howell snorted. 'Useless rubbish. Movement doesn't even fit the case. Austrian factory stuff that's ticked its last tick.'

He turned away. 'Come on. Wasting our time. I shoulda known.'

'You wanted a day out, that's what,' Doran reminded him. 'And I wanted – oh, I don't know what any more. A picture, perhaps. Yes, a picture, for Kit's room. Nothing classy, just an interesting print or a local primitive. Let's go and have a look, now that we're here.'

The pictures, an unpromising array, were hung or propped up in a separate small room. Instantly recognizable were those painted for chain stores, reproduced in their thousands in tasteful oilette effect. The Blue Grotto, Capri, Venice in all her aspects, improbable cottage garden scenes of rustic bliss being shared by dogs, cats, ducks and sunbonneted maidens; inscrutable oriental females and vulgarly behaved Parisian gamins,

24

basked, brooded or frolicked for the delectation of some-body or other.

Doran put on the glasses she only needed for occasional reading and inspected the catalogue closely.

'I don't see anything answering to some of these descriptions. Where's Head of Edwardian Lady?'

Howell pointed to a badly drawn and crudely coloured portrait of a young woman whose piled-up hair and high collar faintly suggested the years before World War One.

'Oh, that,' Doran dismissed it. 'Copy of a postcard? Actress? Someone's grandmother? There doesn't seem to be anything here I'd even want for a garage . . .'

But she had broken off, and bent forward suddenly, taking off her glasses.

'Howell!'

'*Diw!* You made me jump. What's the matter, some-thing bite you?'

'Come and look at this.'

A small, oblong picture of a girl, half-length, done in oil, long enough ago for it to have become darkened and discoloured. Doran picked it up. The frame was a nondescript oak one, unpolished and without a mount. It seemed at first glance that the medium was oil.

The girl leaned against a tree, as though she had walked a long way and needed a rest. Her face was longish, pale, perfect, the eyes cast down beneath singularly heavy lids, the mouth soft, virginal, serious. Hair of a copper-gold that shone out of the grime of the picture, completely straight, centre-parted, lay over one shoulder of the drab, loose tunic she wore.

'Not very sexy,' was all Howell's comment. 'Who dressed her – Oxfam? *Missed another bloody Bus*, I'd call that.'

'Would you? I'd call it Lizzie Siddal. You know, Rossetti's inspiration. The Blessed Damozel.'

25

Howell peered again. 'You mean it's right? OK?' He glanced at Doran. 'Funny colour you've gone, gal.'

From being as pale as the girl in the picture, Doran's cheeks were suddenly flushed pink.

'I've got to have this, Howell,' she said. 'I don't care who else wants it, I've got to have it.'

From the look of things, nobody present was likely to want it at all. The few other dealer types had glanced in and gone out again, to drift away disappointed in their cars. Howell didn't blame them. Fretfully, he prowled round, thinking of lunch and his favourite pubs in the locality.

Doran stayed unmoving, entranced before Lizzie Siddal. And Lizzie, if it were she, stared mournfully past her into infinity.

Sam Eastry's garden was a picture of what a garden should be in September. It was, to his great satisfaction, twice the size of the one he had cultivated before thankfully taking early retirement from the police.

It hadn't worked out, deserting Abbotsbourne for plain-clothes duties amid the squalor and periodic violence to be encountered even in a comparatively staid seaside town. He had come to hate every minute of it. It wasn't what police work had been in his long spell as Abbotsbourne's community cop.

But now he was back, living in a mellow old cottage in the heart of the village he loved. His wife, Lydia, was happy to be among her own friends again. Their boy, Ben, was twenty, past the punk stage which had been an especially difficult one for a policeman's son, egged on by some others to such things as stealing motorbikes and smoking pot in houses awaiting demolition. Ben had a job now, his hair grown to a reasonable length, and he had turned civil at last to his young sister, Jennifer, who was a little older than Kit Chelmarsh and went to the same village school.

Sam glanced out of the window. No real temptation to work in the garden today, in this cold rain. He returned to the pages of a book the former vicar had given him in recognition of his services as captain of St Crispin's bellringers, the proud place he now occupied again. It was *The Bells of England*, written the best part of a hundred years before, and full of antiquarian lore.

It reminded him of Doran, and he smiled. She had welcomed him back so warmly, her old friend and adviser, in a way her father-figure. He hoped she wouldn't get herself into any more trouble with murders. Without looking for it, she had managed to have as much of it as many professional detectives ever did in their whole career. But you never knew with Doran.

At any rate, it wouldn't concern him – officially – any more.

CHAPTER TWO

In the golden light, late the following afternoon, Doran unveiled her prize to Rodney and Kit. She had brought it home triumphantly, having gone back alone for the auction itself that morning, rather than leave a bid and trust to luck.

'What do you think of her?' she asked Kit, who was quite accustomed by now to pronouncing on his mother's new stock.

'She looks tired.'

'Yes, that was the first thing I thought. Anything else?'

'Oh, dunno. Oh, yes – as if she didn't have much to say. Somebody told her to keep quiet.'

'Very good,' Rodney congratulated him. 'Artists' models aren't suppose to chatter.'

'Do you think she's pretty?' Doran insisted.

'Mm. Not very. Not as pretty as Miss Martin.' His new teacher held strong fascination for Kit. Now he wandered away, with no further judgement to pass on Mummy's new picture. But he could see she was excited about it for some reason. That was nice: good to have a Mummy who wasn't always going on like some others about eating and clothes, and playschools, and how much you'd learnt, and who your friends were.

Vi, looking in with her anorak on, ready for going home, paused to give her assessment.

'Not very smart, is she? What's she got on? Looks like a man's coat over her blouse. Meant to be dressed as a boy, is she? Of course, you can't tell nowadays. You speak to one of 'em and a different voice comes out. Is it worth a lot, Miss Doran?'

She still addressed her so; and me a married woman and mother, Doran thought. Rodney was perfectly used to hearing his wife referred to by Vi as though they were living in sin.

'I don't know, Vi,' Doran replied. 'I shan't, until I've examined it carefully. Perhaps not even then.' She was longing to get on with it, hoping Vi wouldn't embark on one of her long disquisitions on the life and manner of girls nowadays. But mercifully Vi wanted to get home in time for the episode of one of her favourite TV soaps.

Doran and Rodney were alone with the prize. Avidly she removed the frame with screwdriver and pliers, and prised out the backing card which held the picture in place. She removed the picture gently and stood holding it. Rodney said nothing, letting her savour the moment.

'It's been out before,' she said at last. 'The frame's oldish, but I'd say it's been on, oh, twenty, thirty years. And it's a slice-up.'

'Not a frame-up?' Rodney suggested.

She was too intent to groan. 'No, the picture. Cut down from a much bigger one. Group composition, perhaps. Pity. It brings down the value a good deal. But if it's the part with the signature on . . .'

Glasses on, she was searching the bottom corners. She got her magnifying lens and peered harder. Rodney sent up a swift prayer that she might find something that would make her happy. She laid the lens aside and took off her spectacles, to use a jeweller's loupe, held in one eye like a monocle. It gave enormous magnification. Rodney saw her disappointed frown.

'Nothing?'

'Nothing. Hell, multiple damnation, blast – anything you can think of that I shouldn't say.'

'What should the signature be? "Rossetti"?'

'A logogram. His initials, DGR, and the date. About 1851, I'd guess. Oh, how hideously disappointing. I *know* it's a Rossetti. I'm sure.'

Rodney was sadly familiar with instances of Doran's knowing works to be by masters, but finding they weren't. 'Could it be,' he suggested gently, ' "School of ", or "After"? Or just a copy?'

She shook her head impatiently. 'Could be, but isn't. He didn't enjoy oil-painting. Too lush, or gooey, or something. So he laid it on as sparingly as he could. Look at this, no lumps or layers built up; just a light coat of paint, used thinly, to seem almost transparent, like watercolour. Typical. A copyist wouldn't imitate that technique, would they? Anyway, if this is a copy, I don't know of the original.'

'Neither do I.' Rodney's taste in pictures lay in the realm of the fantastic, particularly the wild paint- dreaming of Richard Dadd and the rich bizarrerie of Fuseli. In their early days Doran had persuaded him to take such things off his study walls when Church dignitaries were due to call. He had obeyed to humour her, but had never agreed that his mad fairies could have a corruptive influence on anyone; not even Church dignitaries. He found the Pre-Raphaelites, on the whole, too solid, with their ponderous and earthy ways with angels, portraying them as heavily built, over-draped, and with an unfortunate taste for carrying large, depressing lilies.

'But we will soon find the original, if it exists,' he added, with a gleefully anticipatory glance towards the art volumes which made part of his enormous library. 'We will have a Research . . .'

'Oh, yes!'

The evening time after supper stretched delightfully before them. One of the chief joys of life, they agreed, if you were a certain sort of person, was to look something up in as many reference books as possible until you found the truth about it. Shared, the pleasure was doubled.

Doran had her own art books. Combined with Rodney's they covered a long table and much of the floor.

'There's richness!' he crowed. 'You take that end, and we'll meet in the middle.'

The black cat, Tybalt, entered, to register objection to his chair in front of the fire being occupied by a book. Doran removed it obediently. Tybalt gave the vacated seat a contemptuous look and stalked across to the table, where he leapt on to a lushly bound, rare volume, and settled on it with arms folded. She knew better than to lift him off. He would only be back.

They did meet eventually in the middle, but without result at either end. Rodney had been over-optimistic in saying they would soon find a reproduction of the original picture. Among all Rossetti's pictures, not one showed up of a girl leaning against a tree. Rodney straightened and arched his back.

'My spine is beginning to crack like machine-gun fire. I'm going to have a beer. Did you know there was a thick fur coat of dust on some of these books?'

'It collects, however thoroughly one cleans. And Vi does, but I think she has a sort of reverent horror of touching these. At least they're not harbouring disgusting old cobwebs and flat spiders. Yes, please, I *will* have a beer.'

He fetched them some from the kitchen, then settled luxuriously into his armchair. Doran stayed on the floor, flicking over pages.

'Then, do we go on slogging through the Pre-Raphs?' she said.

'By all means. It's a pleasure. Like eating pounds and pounds of something agreeable with garlic in it. One ultimately feels deliciously satisfied but slightly nauseated. They were a rum lot, the Pre-Raphs.'

Doran kicked off her slippers and prepared for one of his meditations.

'The trouble was,' he mused, 'this idea of theirs that their mission in life was to purify art and put it back to what it had been before Raphael, whatever they imagined that was. They wanted to take out all the Georgian stiffness and formalism that they thought had ruled it too long.'

'That's right,' Doran agreed. 'They called Joshua Reynolds "Sir Sloshua", poor man.'

'So they started painting in a different way. Unfortunately – I say this outside my clerical instruction – they thought religion had to be their main ingredient. They weren't religious chaps themselves, but, being Victorians, they had to pose as such. They used allegory, which most people didn't understand. The dastardly Holman Hunt, for instance.'

'So he was. *The Scapegoat*. It looks so wretched and frightened. As well it might, when you think how many poor goats he starved to get his effect. And his public didn't even get the message, did they?'

'He took it for granted that they would – the goat driven out of the Temple on the Day of Atonement, to carry the people's sins away. Rough on the goat, and pretty useless as sin-transport. Likewise, he meant *The Hireling Shepherd* to show that the Church was full of lazy pastors. But all people saw was a trollopish peasant girl on the point of getting seduced by a lout in rope leggings. This isn't getting us anywhere with Rossetti, is it?'

'No, tiresome man.' Doran batted dust off another book, and sneezed. 'They were all mixed up, but he was the mixed-uppest of the lot. Half Italian, full of Latin hormones – the type who drives round Rome blowing

33

his hooter and crashing traffic lights. But the son of a pious English mother. No wonder he grew up seeing women as either tarts or saints.'

'And awkward for Lizzie Siddal.'

'Fatal. Poor Lizzie. Working girl at a milliner's. Polite and nicely behaved. Picked up by one of the Pre-Raphs as one of their ideal Stunners, with red-gold hair, and thin enough figures to suit medieval gowns. Yes, a born victim, Lizzie.'

'Millais' *Ophelia*, wasn't she? I've kept coming across it all evening. Floating in that stream, singing snatches of old songs as she dies.'

'Not a stream, though. A bath in Millais' studio, and the water heated by a lamp underneath – until wretched Millais went out and forgot, and the lamp went out too. Lizzie in that heavily embroidered dress, lying there obediently and getting icier and icier. She got pneumonia, and her father sued – successfully.'

Rodney turned pages until they were looking at the girl in the bath: pale face, pearl-encrusted bodice, hands outspread, the wonderful copper hair floating on the surface like weed.

' "Beautiful as the reflection of a golden mountain on a crystal lake",' read Rodney. 'That's what Ruskin said she was to Rossetti. He was the mountain, Lizzie the lake.'

'But the mountain burnt the lake up, in the end. It took him ten years to get round to marrying her, and by then she was hooked on laudanum and more or less fed up with Dante Gabriel and his lifestyle. So she died, probably suicide, after bearing a dead baby.' Doran shuddered. She'd known about the baby before; about Lizzie being found by a visitor, sitting in a chair with the cradle on the floor beside her. 'Hush, Ned, you'll waken it,' she'd said.

34

Rodney had been reading on. 'And then that ghastly Highgate Cemetery business – Dante Gabriel having her dug up to get the manuscript of his poems out of her coffin. Still legible, though her hair had gone on growing round it. They had the manuscript disinfected, of course.'

'How gratifying!' Doran's face was as pale as Ophelia's as she went on staring at her painting. Gently, Rodney took it out of her hands.

'That's enough about Lizzie Siddal tonight.' Time to switch tracks and distract her mind with nonsense. 'I've had enough of the Pre-Raphaelites, after an evening on them. My prize for the world's most boring picture would go easily to *Chaucer at the Court of Edward III*. Closely followed by *Work*, or, *How to Behave with Absolute Uselessness in Hampstead*. Sooner watch endless catfood commercials.'

Doran wasn't listening. Now that Rodney had made up the fire, the painting glowed where she had put it down.

'I got it for twelve pounds,' she mused. 'The auctioneer started it at five, and only two other people were bidding. Not real dealers, of course. Hardly surprising, and nobody in the trade's going to give me much profit on an unsigned slice-up. Ah, well, it's a nice thing to have – I think.'

Rodney thought otherwise. The sad, too-thin model reminded him of Doran when he had first known her; a well-educated, ethereally pretty waif with no clue to the geography of life. Like Lizzie Siddal, she hadn't known where or who she was. He wished the picture hadn't turned up to reincarnate that waif; especially at a time when she often looked too thin and pale herself for his liking.

Perhaps it would help to be constructive.

'Can I mention this thing in my column?' he suggested.

'Such as, the other day my wife made a discovery which may throw a shaft of light on the world of Victorian art . . .'

Doran hesitated, before saying, 'Well, all right. If you want.'

It was a decision that was to have a far-reaching, deadly outcome.

CHAPTER THREE

The weeks passed; the leaves fell in the first days of that benevolent October. Sniffing the aromatic smoke from garden bonfires, Doran saw in her mind, over and over again, the haunting Millais painting *Autumn Leaves*. Four solemn, melancholy-eyed young girls, two of them black-clad, as if mourning for the summer, pouring dead leaves on to the growing heap at their feet. Inky clouds spreading across the sunset sky. A feeling of mystery, apprehension . . .

There was no getting away from those Pre-Raphaelites, it seemed.

'They're the only field I'd really love to specialize in,' she told Howell at the Port Arms one weekend. 'They seem to have taken me over, since I found that picture.'

He snorted. 'Seen the auction prices, have you? Know the great collections that's collared most of them – the Tate, Manchester, Birmingham, Liverpool? Not to mention rich foreigners. You win the pools first, then you might get to buy a broken-off bit of frame. Forget it.'

'Thanks, but I can't. If my one of Lizzie has escaped, there could be others around still. Who knows how many they painted and what became of every single one? Suppose I were to track down all the places where they lived and worked? I might be able to trace families that knew them and could have got bequests . . .'

Howell's tomcat moustache twitched with his impatience.

'Your Lizzie's no more Rossetti than I am. Anyway,

just stop and think, will you? Who's goin' to run your shop, and go out buying stock for you? Where were you thinking of goin' lookin'?'

'Oxfordshire. Morris's Kelmscott's still there. Chelsea, where Rossetti lived so long . . .'

'Never noticed that Chelsea's changed a bit since his day, when it was a kind of village? Noticed there's a thing called telvision that people watch, and makes 'em wonder how much that old picture of Auntie's that they never liked might be worth? You've done a Roadshow yourself. Come on, grow up, *merch*.'

He saw the droop of Doran's mouth, and knew that she really did care about her mad idea, and felt cast down by his swift demolition of it. Unreasonably cast down.

'Here,' he said suspiciously, 'you're not gettin' funny, are you? Like before?'

'Funny? Before? Before what?'

He was suddenly coy. '*You* know. Touchy. Tears and violins. All that. Women's stuff.'

'Oh!' It was Doran's turn to blush, right up to her brow. She put her hands to her face. In his way, Howell had always admired her looks, especially that boyish cap of curly hair. She'd let it grow now, so that it straggled down to her shoulders. Unbecomingly, he thought. And even his not very expert eye for such things noted a faint reddish tinge to it – been using a rinse, silly cow. Probably spotted a grey hair. Women, they couldn't stand that. Look at his Mam, black as a crow at going on seventy, all out of bottles. Neurotic, they were.

'You think I may have started fancying Pre-Raphaelites instead of strange fruits, or unobtainable shellfish, or tripe and onions?' she said.

'Somethin' like that. Sorry, didn't mean to be nosy.'

'No, it isn't that. At least, I don't think so. I wish it were.'

38

Howell ostentatiously picked up the glossy catalogue he'd been scanning while waiting for her to turn up. His thought about his mother had transmitted itself to Doran. She thought of her, too, wishing she'd suddenly materialize beside them: magical Gwenllian, as Welsh as Owain Glyn Dwr, as exotically clad as a bird of paradise, as all-capable as Mary Poppins. Gwenllian had solved problems for Doran before. She would understand now, say the right things, turn one's thoughts in the right direction . . .

'What's Gwenllian doing these days?' she asked Howell.

The echo of his own thought startled him briefly. 'Mam? Gone off on a cruise. Tobago, or somewhere.'

'Oh. Pity.'

He didn't bother to ask why. 'Never mind Mam. I'd forgotten what I was going to ask you. Come to a party next Tuesday? Guy at Bartleby's. Top brass. Does himself well. Dunno why he invited me.'

'Where?'

'London. Place in Kensington.'

Howell did know why he'd been asked, and also why his colleague had invited him to bring a girl; someone on the safe side, who could be relied on not to poach. Doran fitted the bill, being unlikely to favour any of the colleague's particular male friends, though she had a strong leaning towards a certain type – for preference grey-haired and spectacled.

So it was that on an early November night she was thoughtfully sipping her third glass of wine, and gazing with approval through a window spangled with rain at a storm-lashed Kensington. The street lamps were strongly bright, reflected in soaked pavements and the windows of passing taxis. It made her think of the sort of old film that Rodney found compulsive. At any moment that man waiting to cross the road might turn into Hitchcock himself making his token appearance in one of his movies. An old-fashioned bobby on the beat would pass by gravely, the rain streaming down his waterproof cape. She felt, in the black skirt and white top that she usually rather disliked, that it was a scene into which she fitted visually rather well.

It was exciting to be on the loose in London. Exciting to be in a crowd of chattering, drinking strangers, all seeming to know each other, but none except Howell knowing her. Close by, a foreign-looking girl in thick glasses, wearing a long puce kaftan and earrings down to her shoulders, was chatting familiarly with a wispy fair young man and a neat-suited older one, with Expert written all over him. As he gestured while he spoke, Doran noticed the Expert's well-manicured hands, the sort which look so well in television close-ups, handling delicate porcelain without the least likelihood of ever dropping any. In the near distance was a group of girls in designer jeans, and young men who looked like actors: the party host, she recognized, surrounded by his retinue. All strangers to her.

Never mind. The wine was unusually good for this sort of thrash. She and Howell had come up by train, so there was no need to observe discretion about drinking and driving home. Just as well, judging from Howell's raised voice, telling a prolonged story that sounded as if it wouldn't have suited Abbotsbourne society. He was in the group around their host, a large amiable, glossy young man, surprisingly young, it seemed to Doran, for the high post he held at Bartleby's. But then, it was a young man's world now, everyone knew that.

She turned her back on the rainy night outside, and her own reflection in the window, to survey the room. It was the double salon of a house that probably went up about the time that the young Victoria vowed to be good, not two miles from this spot. According to tradition, anyway. Would a normal, healthy girl say such a thing, roused virtually at dawn to be told her king-uncle was dead, so she was queen? Wouldn't it have been more natural to ask her ministers if they'd breakfasted, and ring for early tea in any case?

A voice dispelled the misty vision of Kensington Palace. Doran emerged from it, aware that the voice was asking if she were bored.

'What an interesting question,' was her reaction. 'I hope I don't seem it.'

She was looking at a woman rather shorter than herself and considerably plumper: a head of short dandelion-clock hair, which might be either platinum-fair or prematurely silver. Bright blue eyes were watching her inquisitively, yet kindly, as though their owner really meant her question.

'I didn't mean to disturb you,' said the woman; 'but I thought perhaps you had no-one to talk to. Parties are so peculiar, aren't they? Not really as friendly as they're made out to be. But now I've disturbed you, anyway. Sorry.'

She was turning away, but Doran stopped her. 'Don't go. I wasn't actually bored. I was daydreaming, and I shouldn't, not at parties. I don't know anyone here, in fact – except Howell Evans.'

The blue eyes sparkled. 'Howell Evans! He's why I'm here. I do a bit of valuing for Bartleby's, and met him, and he asked me.'

'How amazing! He's practically my best friend.'

Doran thought that, for a comparative new boy at the firm, Howell seemed to be making free with the invitations. But one never knew with Howell. They talked about him, always a fertile subject, and then about a tapestry Bartleby's had just auctioned for a monumental sum. Her new acquaintance was knowledgeable on tapestries.

A waitress paused to refill their glasses. Doran, conversationally fuelled by the wine, found that she was enjoying talking to this cheerful creature, who seemed to be on her wavelength, certainly in the field of textiles, which she said was her speciality. They found they shared a passion for fine needlework, samplers, richly wrought garments from the past, stumpwork to cushion jewel boxes, great tapestries, and American quilts, like fields of magic flowers. The subject of pictures, so much on Doran's mind lately, came to the surface of it, and, to her lips, the name Rossetti. But even the wine didn't overcome her dealer's instinct not to say more. It was unwise, against the rules of good sense, to reveal a new find and one's current interest in a special field.

And something else, in this case – a curious guilt, a sort of shame, as though one were about to drag the name of a lover into casual conversation. No. Keep Dante Gabriel and Lizzie to yourself, Doran.

She mentioned instead her prized collection of fans. The other woman's eyes opened wide.

'You've really got a collection? Oh, how I envy you. Are any of them haunted?'

The question wasn't one to surprise a true collector. 'Two or three,' Doran replied readily. 'A French Revolution one I keep by itself, so it can't frighten the others. And a late nineteenth-century silk painted thing that has no right to be sinister, but is, somehow. The only fans I've never wanted to collect are those horrible obscenities trimmed with bits of exotic birds – humming birds' heads, and of course, the gigantic swansdown Parisian.

Do you know it? Swan, stuffed and surrounded by its own feathers. How frightful.'

Her new friend's face seemed to have turned a shade paler. 'Don't,' she said faintly. 'Don't tell me any horrors, or they'll spoil my evening.'

'I feel exactly the same,' Doran assured her. 'I'm sorry I mentioned that one. Come and see my fans some time.'

The other recovered instantly. 'I'd love that. Could I really? Wouldn't it be a bore for you?'

'Not at all, though I don't live in town. Down in remotest Kent.'

'Well, I'm at Blackheath. It used to be Kent before they dragged it into London.'

Doran was surprised to find that she'd meant her invitation; she who issued so few invitations to the refuge of her home. So often they hadn't worked. Rodney liked his privacy in the evenings, after his days filled with dealing with other people. This one, she was sure, would work, but a thought struck her belatedly.

'It's ridiculous, but we haven't introduced ourselves.'

'Nor we have. Mine's a very odd name – Ancilla Ireland. Ancilla.' She spelt it out. 'Pronounced with a k.'

'That's very unusual,' agreed Doran, whose own name wasn't exactly commonplace. 'I've never come across one before. Is it a family name?'

'No, just mine.'

'It reminds me of something, though. I can't think what. Never mind. I'm Doran Chelmarsh. Fairweather, to the trade, but I prefer to use my husband's name.'

They exchanged addresses. Ancilla told her she had a flat in a solid though ugly Edwardian house. She did her antiques trading from it.

'Unobtrusively, though. Landlords are inclined to be prohibitive if they find out one's doing business on domestic premises.'

43

They left it as a date to be arranged, then someone beckoned Ancilla from across the room and she excused herself and went to join them. She left Doran with a sense of warmth. She wasn't beautiful, or even pretty, but she seemed to give out a kind of radiance, Doran thought. Odd, if Howell's invitation to them both resulted in their becoming friends.

Drifting in the opposite direction, now nicely lubricated, Doran got into easy conversation with another guest standing alone, a girl with punk hair and jeans, who proved to be erudite about netsuke, but who departed abruptly when Doran observed that ivory carvings ought to be banned. After a few more unsatisfactory attempts at conversation, Doran found the letdown that could follow wine's stimulus beginning to creep over her. She realized her shoes were hurting, she was tired, and it was getting late. She managed to extricate Howell, who didn't seem entirely pleased.

On the train home he was more inclined to sleep than to talk. Doran didn't mind. She was glad of his company in the cold, unsavoury carriage, littered with plastic cups and food wrappings, and populated by furtive-eyed people who seemed to move restlessly to and fro, sinister extras in a film that was no longer enjoyable.

Perhaps he felt she'd dragged him away too early; when he did pay attention to her he affected vagueness. That woman Ireland? Ann, her name was, as far as he knew. No, she wasn't a pal of his. He may have mentioned the party to her, but it wouldn't have been his place to invite her, would it? Some freeloaders would go anywhere at the hint of a bottle and a few bits of prawn . . .

Doran gave him up to his sleep. She sat back and reflected on Ancilla's remembered charm, picturing that bright changing face in the train's dark windows.

Ancilla, Pronounced with a k, Ankilla. What did it

make her think of? Of course – inevitably – Dante Gabriel Rossetti, and his early painting *Ecce Ancilla Domini* – Behold the Handmaid of the Lord.

Extraordinary.

CHAPTER FOUR

Rodney lifted the heavy latch of the door of St Crispin's Church. It was unlocked for once and he went inside. The interior of the beautiful old building where he had once been vicar was dark and gloomy, even on this bright, delusory November morning. Somehow it looked less old and beautiful than it had done in his time. Vanity, he rebuked himself. Never mind; it was St Luke's Day, and he must light a candle.

There were no lights on, of course. Flowers were in front of the lectern, as usual, and on a small modern table he didn't remember. But they were hardly a blaze of colour: their arranger had settled for brown and gold chrysanthemums, which almost disappeared in the shadows.

He turned into the Lady Chapel, carefully keeping his eyes from the altar where the medieval reredos had stood, and from an extremely depressing charity poster which had replaced an undistinguished but pleasant Nativity. Worthy, very proper, but not in the right place. It belonged over by the south door, where the notices and literature were.

He stopped. The object he had been looking for was not there. The candlestand, which in his time had been a fine little constellation of tiny flames, was gone, as was the box for money. Ten pence a candle, it had been: just something nominal for the fabric restoration fund.

His first feeling of shock was replaced by disgust at his

47

own forgetfulness. How absent-minded can you get, you old fool? At that moment another voice spoke aloud behind him.

'Looking for something, Rodney?'

The Reverend Edwin Dutton's only sartorial concession to his calling was a clerical collar. Otherwise he was dressed for something like inspecting gas meters. He had emerged from the vestry, moving silently on the carpet of the aisle.

'No,' replied Rodney. 'At least, yes, but I ought to have remembered. I dropped in to light a candle to St Luke, and completely forgot there aren't any candles these days.'

Edwin Dutton smiled thinly. This was his church now.

'Not since just after I came here, in fact. A little High, I felt. But then, you know my feelings, Rodney, and you've certainly never hidden yours. Never mind. Both well, are you? And Christopher?'

'Yes, fine, thanks.'

'Doran still going in to Eastgate? I saw her yesterday, driving out of the village. You know, when she decides to give it up I can find her some very, very useful work. Celia is extremely active in the Deprived People movement, as you know, and she needs helpers. Making collections, photocopying, addressing envelopes, all that sort of thing.'

'I'm sure she does. But I don't think Doran intends to give up the shop. It's an important part of her life. Not to mention our living.'

The church clock struck portentously.

'Good gracious, is that the time?' Rodney heard himself coming out with the old, old line. But it would get him away. With Edwin Dutton, he always seemed to babble. 'Have to rush, I'm afraid. I was in the middle of doing some of the Saturday shopping when it occurred to me about St Luke. Memory lapse about the candles, though . . .'

He had got as far as the nave, almost escaped, but the vicar's relentless voice caught up with him.

'And by the way, Rodney, we don't really make a great *point* of saints in the modern, realistic Church of England. Very worthy, many of them, I'm sure. Really splendid people in some cases. But there's always the slight danger of superstitious practices and the deflection of worship. We need to be quite sure of the candidate's absolute qualifications before making a special case for promoting a quite, er, ordinary human being to such a height.'

Rodney choked back a famous quotation from St Augustine. Instead he said, 'I'd have thought St Luke, being a doctor, a brilliant chronicler, and a great teacher – not to mention a personal friend of Our Lord – qualified as rather more than a quite ordinary human being. However . . .'

He escaped swiftly. In the churchyard he ran, more than walked, to the car.

At Bell House, Doran, frying pan in hand, stared as Rodney threw the carrier bags from the Indian supermarket on to the kitchen floor. An ominous clink and crash suggested that the contents were suffering.

'What on earth . . . ?'

'That man, Dutton,' he seethed. 'He's a fiend. A bane. A blight. A sepulchre, and not even a whited one.' He gave her a brief rundown of the conversation in the church.

'Why does he bring out the worst in me? I've been in orders longer than he has. I'm probably better educated. I'm certainly level with him in theology. Yet I can't talk to him without babbling nervously and having to show off. What is he, after all? An ex-maths teacher. "Woe is me, that I am constrained to dwell with Mesech, and to have my habitation among the tents of Kedar. My soul hath long dwelt among them that are enemies unto peace." There, now I'm showing off even to you.'

'Not at all. I know exactly how you feel. Sit down, calm down, and have a drink. I hope there's some wine left in those carriers.' But, as she spoke, a trickle of pale liquid, widening, spread from its brown paper wrapping and began to follow the slope of the floor.

'Oh no! It's going under the dishwasher. Quick – mop it up!'

Between them they arrested the growing flood, took out the broken bottle, and salvaged the carrier's other contents.

'Such a nice unpretentious little wine,' mourned Rodney. 'Only two pounds eighty and the last bottle they had. Gone, and never called me father. That'll teach me for my nasty savage temper.'

'Edwin Dutton would put Patient Griselda in a nasty savage temper,' she consoled him. 'Though you sound to have been very moderate with him. Let's go and find a church where you *can* light a candle this afternoon. Where do you suggest?'

Rodney thought it was an ironical situation for an ex-vicar to be in, unemployed at the weekend, idly going out candle-seeking; but her suggestion had diverted his attention to reviewing other nearby churches.

'St Anselm's is very Anglo, but it'll be locked, unless there's a wedding this afternoon. Trinity . . . ? He plays golf every Saturday. We could go as far as Stoner, to St George's, or, of course, just settle for Barminster and Rome.'

'And I could do some shopping.' Doran's tone was absent-minded, as though her thoughts weren't truly on goods from the Pantry Shelf or the Barminster Centre,

50

where presents could be got well before the Christmas rush.

Rodney looked at her over the top of his spectacles.

'You're working up to something. Something you want to say, but I might not like. Right?'

'Right. Nothing awful, just a suggestion.' She twisted a thread that Tybalt's claws had teased loose from her woollen skirt. 'Just that – Rossetti, if I might mention the name – spent a sort of holiday in Kent in 1878, or thereabouts. Not that he ever spent a proper holiday anywhere. He went to get over one of his spells of illness. He and Ford Madox Brown came down together and stayed in a cottage near Herne Bay.'

'Now take a deep breath,' Rodney counselled gently. 'That wasn't too bad, was it? I do realize you're fascinated by the Rossettis.'

'But you don't think I'm obsessive? I always seem to be talking about the wretched man. It's not that I admire him, I think he was a selfish, sexist, hypocritical beast, especially to Lizzie. I don't even like his painting style too much. I can't explain, really.'

'No need. I do understand.'

'You always do. I might have known. So you wouldn't mind if we went over to Herne Bay after lunch?'

'I'd enjoy it. It would take me a safe distance from Edwin Dutton and my only chance to make headlines in the Sunday press, "Former vicar attacks successor. Blunt instrument. Mayhem in church." No, let's go to Herne Bay on the trail of Dante Gabriel, by all means.'

Doran's kiss, even after their years of marriage, was the real thing.

Offered the chance of an afternoon out with his parents, Kit shook his head. 'I'm going to play with Paul. His Dad's got some new puppies and he's taking us to the kennels to see them. I can, can't I?'

'Oh, darling, yes. Puppies are lovely, and after all it isn't the dogs' fault.'

Rodney and Kit understood what she meant. Her loathing of blood sports stopped short of condemning the animals who were trained to pursue and kill other animals. Paul's Dad's puppies would undoubtedly be reared to that, but lovely in themselves.

'I'm glad you don't go on about it to him,' Rodney said when Kit had left them. 'Over-pressurized, he could easily grow up into a dedicated MFH.'

'There must be more to that than childhood influences,' Doran replied. 'Curious, about this conversation, in view of where we're going. It's a place called Hunters Forstal.'

There was not, they agreed, anything about the small outcrop of Herne Bay to suggest that it had once been a meeting point of local huntsmen. Nor that Rossetti had had any influence on it, or it on him. There were cottages, but none with apparent post-Pre-Raphaelite undertones, or a plaque.

'A less Rossettian place I've never seen,' Rodney pronounced. 'Are you sure he stayed here?'

'Certain.'

'Why?'

'I've no idea. He was full of chloral at the time, so presumably it didn't matter to him where he was. In fact, he got worse here.'

'Not surprisingly. Nothing against the place, but the whole area isn't exactly one of awesome grandeur or pastoral lushness, is it? In fact, why don't we go back and enjoy Herne Church?'

'Must we?' They had dropped in at several churches already, questing in vain for candles, and Doran was growing faintly tired of it. 'Kit will be home by half past four, and I don't want him to have to wait in the garden for us.'

Rodney sighed. 'Ruskin said the tower was one of the few perfect things in the world. There are some good brasses, too – one of Ridley's friend Lady Fineux, "that godly woman there" he called her, more or less on his way to the flames of Oxford. Did you know Herne was where he first arranged for the Te Deum to be sung in English? Revolutionary for those times, and it led to . . .'

'Have you mentioned that in your radio talks?' Doran interrupted him hastily. 'If not, I think you should. No, we won't go back to Herne, because I want to see where Dante Gabriel died and is buried, and that's Birchington, the other way.'

The Irish cross of stone, marking the burial place near the south porch of All Saints, Birchington, told any tourists who might be interested that Dante Gabriel Rossetti was honoured among painters as a painter, and among poets as a poet. Inside the church they gazed at the two-light window to Gabriel, paid for by his old mother. The design of half of it was his own.

' "The families of Joseph and Zacharias uniting for the Passover",' Rodney read out. 'Not an incident much dwelt on these days. But I could use it for a sermon.' He scribbled in one of the notebooks which lived in the pockets of any jacket he wore.

Doran stared moodily up at the figures in the window, trying to see Lizzie among the women, or Dante Gabriel's golden-haired mistress, his Monna Vanna and *Bocco Baciata*, the Kissed Mouth. They were absent. She wondered why she had dragged Rodney all this way, into flat Thanet with its now grey-veiled coastline and seaside-suburban overbuilding. It reminded her always of the frightening time when Kit had been abducted –

when she had driven to Ramsgate and danger in quest of the sinister carved Cherub stolen from her.

Why come back now, merely to indulge a silly pre-occupation with a painter and a picture? Not even deliberately seeking anything this time, unless it were a new interest, something to fill her mind. And change the colour of her bank balance. If the painting were only an indisputable Rossetti, that would have been enough.

'Not just the money, though,' she said aloud. Rodney wandered back from inspecting the brasses to the Crispe family. 'You spoke?'

'Only talking to myself. Shall we go?'

Outside, Rodney drew her back towards the grave and the stone cross.

'There,' he said, pointing triumphantly. 'I was sure I'd missed something. The carving on the stem, of the old man and the ox. Why didn't I spot it before?'

Doran glanced at her watch. 'What's special about it?'

'St Luke. The ox is his emblem. Of course – the patron saint of painters. I knew he ought to be here somewhere. Good.' Satisfied, he slipped an arm round her shoulders as they walked back to the car. 'What about your preoccupations now? Has visiting Dante Gabriel's tomb exorcized them?'

'Mm. I don't think so. No. I have a curious feeling that I'm being drawn into something that I don't like very much.'

'You? Wasn't it all rather too long ago for you to be drawn into it now? Or do you feel there's some ghostly element to it?'

'No, no, no,' Doran said emphatically. 'Though Dante Gabriel and Lizzie would make perfect ghosts, wouldn't they? – pale and hollow-eyed and wild. They could do it for a living – I mean professionally. If only all the houses they'd lived in hadn't been pulled down . . . But no, I don't feel they're trying to engage me as public vindicator, or revealer of a secret, or anything. I'm fascinated by them, that's all. The beauty and the poetry, and underneath it something else, something horrible – misunderstandings and guilt, and more than a bit of madness. Guggums, he called her, "wonderful lovely Guggums". And painted her like an icon, with no expression at all.'

'Personally,' said Rodney, putting on his driving gloves as they settled into the car, 'I feel that Dante Gabriel's paintings have all the lure of phosphorescence on dead fish – pretty, but rotten. The drugs, of course. Not really as bad as our own drug scene, because the Victorians didn't know what they were doing to themselves, taking laudanum for everything from toothache to tetanus.'

He hoped, driving south-westwards into the low wintry sunset, that Doran would get over it soon. An obsession, he agreed, and an unhealthy one. He had never pressed her to work at the rôle of vicar's wife, and certainly didn't intend doing so now that Abbotsbourne wasn't even within his parish. But, he thought wistfully, there were so many useful and satisfying things she could be doing, instead of brooding over the mixed-up lives of dead artists' models. Perhaps he should have done as Edwin Dutton advised, and directed her towards Good Works.

His Doran. So intelligent, so knowledgeable about her trade, so mature in many ways – and yet . . . He knew there was an imbalance in her, something that wasn't mature at all. Whatever it might be, it gave her a need of father-figures: older men such as Howell and Sam Eastry. Howell had gone from her now, and Sam no longer had a local bobby's paternal authority. They had left a cold space where they had been. Rodney hoped that the remarkably non-fatherly shade of Dante Gabriel Rossetti wasn't trying to fill it.

Ridiculous, of course, considering that Rodney himself was much older than she. But, painfully self-analytical, he saw himself as a flawed person. He knew his own weakness only too well: pedantry, depending too much on the spoken and written word, with too little commitment to the world and its people outside his family.

'We're going for a walk tomorrow,' he said decisively. 'This musing on epitaphs is all very well, but you need some proper exercise. So do I – I expect. Let's follow the river.'

Before Kit was born their favourite walk had been along the banks of the little river Leddon from the point where it appeared, somewhat furtively, from behind a disused mill and derelict railway sheds beyond the station, flowed sedately through the valley, built itself up into a mini-waterfall in wet weather, then gently meandered off through open country to the coast. But when Kit had been a toddler in a pushchair the walk wasn't so attractive, with its frequently over-narrow paths; and somehow the river path had become neglected by them.

Doran knew that Rodney was not excessively fond of walking. He was growing more and more sedentary, happiest with his books and his sheaves of notes on remarkable and eccentric features of Kentish ecclesiastical architecture. He was making this suggestion for her good alone. She would be properly grateful.

'All right, we're going for a walk. I shall like that.'

Rodney thought that he would quite like it, too. The Rossettis could hardly come for a walk with them.

Sunday afternoon proved grey, cold and damp. It would have been much nicer to stay in. But Kit was invited to the home of yet another friend, and there was really no excuse for lingering round the fire with the Sunday supplements. They walked Kit to his friend's gate in Cow Lane, and saw him inside.

'A full social life, that child leads,' Doran said as they walked on. 'I wonder if it goes on like this, or if they get more and more sort of isolated as they grow older?' That had happened to her, an only child in a North Oxford house where elderly people, or people who seemed elderly to her, formed most of her society. Much better not be an only child . . . The empty cradle. She mustn't think of the empty cradle.

'I should think Kit will always have a fairly packed social life,' Rodney replied. 'He's a good listener. People with that quality never lack friends. Do we have to be conscientious, by the way, and go as far as the mill? It's terribly boring.'

'It may be, but it's the pattern of this walk. We must do it properly or not at all.'

Dutifully, they reached the point where grey, sluggish water slid out past concrete bunkers, wooden sheds and general industrial debris. It looked thoroughly discouraged after its earlier progress at the side of the railway line, as though it had become abashed at even being called a river any longer, and might resign itself to functioning only as a dump for unwanted things. Doran began mentally to compose a limerick about it, based on the words again, strain and drain. It wasn't going to be a very good limerick; she abandoned it with relief as the Leddon perked up beyond the village. From the last field, where desultory sheep pottered, a boy was even fishing.

'You'd have to be a maniac to expect results from that,' Rodney said. 'What's going to rise – hibernating newts, water beetles, worms? Can't fish for worms with worms. Sounds like *Hamlet*. Do you suppose . . .'

He stopped, cutting off a disquisition on Shakespeare's

real reason for having 'Curst be he who moves my bones' as his epitaph. This walk was intended to cheer Doran up and keep her mind off morbidity. Instead, he drew attention to the effect of recent rains, swelling the river from its apologetic trickle to something more impressive.

'Not exactly the way the waters come down at Lodore, as in the poem,' he concluded. 'But at least it looks like a river again. Can we go home now?'

'Certainly not,' Doran refused. 'I want to see the pool. There are little fishes sometimes, and the birds come and drink.'

Rodney managed not to sigh. The expedition wasn't proving much of a success – for him. His knees were aching, as they often did on cold, damp days, and he wished he'd put on his warmer jersey. All those summers of cricket and tennis, he decided, hadn't done a lot to toughen him up for what he considered long-distance walking.

Doran, in her thick woollen coat, its hood firmly pinned to her hair, was perfectly comfortable. Rodney had generously offered her the family deerstalker, but nobly she had refused it in his favour. Not entirely nobly, but partly from reluctance to look like the billionth member of a Sherlock Holmes club. There was such a thing as pride, even in a deserted valley on a dank Sunday afternoon.

The water, on its way to the little natural weir, ran clear at last, looking pure enough to put into a kettle. The thought occurred forcefully to Rodney, with the prospect of half an hour's uphill homeward tramp to the actual kettle and the comfort of a hot drink.

They were almost at the pool below the weir.

'Oh, no!' Doran exclaimed. 'Don't say they've started dumping here, too!'

'Looks like it. Somebody who couldn't be bothered to

knock at our back door and offer their old clothes for the Christmas Fair.'

Doran stopped short, a hand on his arm, staring at something in the stretch of calm water below the stones.

'Except that it isn't just old clothes,' she said tensely.

Rodney's spectacles were spotted with rain. He took them off, wiped them, and resumed them.

Doran heard the catch of breath which in another man would have been Oh God!

Together they ran down the slope to where, half on the grass edge, half in the water, the body lay. There was no doubt at all that it was a corpse, even before they reached it and stared down at the open, blank eyes, the still, stiff hands.

It was Doran who said, 'Oh, God.'

The girl was young – had been young, for now she was ageless. The strange anonymity of the dead had wiped out any character from her white, wet face. Red hair, centre-parted and straight, fell over her shoulders and trailed on the grass. Her dress, cut high in the neck, now a soggy rag, seemed to be made of greyish lace. From the bodice, tight-fitting over small breasts, a sparkle of jewellery caught the light. In one limp hand was a posy of winter flowers, anemones, purple and red, and a miniature yellow chrysanthemum.

'Ophelia,' Doran said, 'Lizzie as Millais' Ophelia.' She heard how her voice shook, as though it were a stranger's. She went on her knees and made herself touch the dead girl's cheek.

Rodney knelt beside her. 'God have mercy on her,' he said, thinking God in his mercy lend her grace; but that was the Lady of Shalott, another dead girl floating on a river: he despised himself for being reminded of that, or any other quotation, at such a moment.

'We must move her,' he said. 'I know the police say

one shouldn't, but we can't leave her in the water like this. At least let's put her on the grass.'

Between them they dragged the heavy weight to lie on the river bank. Like that, she appeared even more dead. But to Doran's relief she was now seen clearly as a real person, crudely dressed as a mock-up of the famous painting. The shoes were modern trainers, the complexion was thickly freckled, as Lizzie Siddal's could never have been; the hair was a natural carroty red, where Lizzie's had been golden-auburn. Now that the dress was out of the water, Doran could see that it had been roughly cobbled together, perhaps from two lengths of lace curtain material, and the glinting jewels were pathetic strips of coloured cabochons, tacked on to look like real gems.

'I thought, for a moment, it was Lizzie herself,' Doran admitted. 'Though how could it have been? Unless it was an optical delusion. Or a ghost . . .'

'None of them,' Rodney said. 'Lizzie's been dead over a century and a quarter. This girl died yesterday, I think.' He had seen many deaths in his years of parish visiting.

'Died? Of natural causes? She got herself up like this, and came to the pool to die?'

'Unlikely. Somebody brought her here.'

'And drowned her? No. If she'd drowned she would look quite different.'

Rodney examined the dead face, the skin texture, the open pale eyes. Then he picked up the hand that held the flowers, noticing with pity and anger that they were tied to it with cotton: Ophelia had never held them of her own choice.

Doran gasped as the inner wrist came into view, then the inside of the elbow, revealed as Rodney gently pushed up the sleeve.

'She was a . . .'

'An addict. For a long time. Punctures all over the other inside arm, too. We must get the police at once. I shouldn't have touched her.'

Doran stood up. 'So she *was* murdered. Somebody killed her, then dressed her up and brought her here. I know that's how it was, whatever they find when they examine her. I *know* it.'

CHAPTER FIVE

There was a telephone box on the fringe of the village. Rodney's 999 call raised the police at Eastgate.

'Yes,' Rodney said into the phone. 'Yes, of course. Yes, we will. Yes.'

Doran held the door wider for him to emerge.

'What did they say? What were you saying to them – all those yeses?'

'They're coming straight out. I said we'd go back there and wait for them. We must.'

Doran nodded. Impossible to leave that poor creature alone by the river in the new heavy rain. Not that it could do her any further harm.

They went back to the pool, where Doran was half surprised to see the body still lying. In thrillers it had always vanished, either because someone had spirited it away or because it hadn't been dead in the first place. Something flew up from it, startling them both unpleasantly – a bird which had been pecking at the flowers in the dead hand.

There was nothing they could do but wait, in the cold rain, uncomfortable sentinels. Doran tried not to look at what they were guarding, but her eyes were drawn back to it again and again. So young, so soon finished. Her own fault, perhaps, as Lizzie's own death, suicide or not, had been, but none the less pitiable. But who in their right senses could have played such a grotesque joke on her body, and brought it here? And why? At least it could have no connection with herself, her obsession. No-one could have known she would come walking this way, to find it.

Doran let herself study the face. Not Lizzie's perfect features, by any means. Not what one might call a refined face; nose too snub, a disproportionate length to the upper lip, the heavy crop of freckles, too many to be attractive. Why? Freckles weren't all that common these days.

Except in outdoor workers. Someone who worked in the open air. Perhaps on a farm? In a garden centre? Possible.

Something else Doran thought she detected. The face was not typically English, if such a thing as an English type existed. Irish – that was it; a red-haired Irish girl, or Scots. A peasant girl, like the one in the *Hireling Shepherd*. For something to pass the time, she tried to visualize the painting, the wench half-lying back in the grass, a vacant-looking lamb on her knee, chewing green apples. A girl silly enough to feed lambs on green apples could be silly enough to feed herself on soft drugs. The drift into hard drugs . . .

Rodney was silently reciting the Thirty-ninth Psalm, the beginning of the Burial Service. He had said the words aloud so many times, yet the solemn language still moved him deeply: 'Man walketh in a vain shadow, and disquieteth himself in vain: he heapeth up riches, and cannot tell who shall gather them . . . When thou with rebukes dost chasten man for sin, thou makest his beauty to consume away, like as it were a moth fretting a garment . . . for I am a stranger with thee, and a sojourner, as all my fathers were.'

Ancient, awesome, familiar words. And they mean all of us – me, Doran, Kit, and this unknown one. Lord, have mercy upon us.

He deliberately shook himself free of the dark cloud. Frivolity, however inapt, might help.

'I've always wondered – had Ophelia been fished out of the stream by the time Gertrude entered to break the news? Or was she still floating in the brook while Gertrude was wittering on about crow-flowers and nettles and daisies, and whatever rude word Tudor shepherds used for long purples? It would have been quite typical of a woman who remarried a month after her husband died – had been murdered, in fact. People do notice these things, especially in royal circles.'

Talking nonsense to fill the silence. Without that, there would be only the distant melancholy hoot of a train and the shriek of gulls, in from the coast, prospecting for inland food. Doran moved protectingly nearer to Ophelia. Rodney continued to speculate on the character of Gertrude, his eyes on the distant road that led to the sea.

Against the grey hillside, far off, flashing blue lights appeared, moving rapidly towards them. Doran breathed deeply with relief.

'They're here. Oh good!' That was putting it mildly. Rodney muttered a silent word of thanks to the power which had expedited the ambulance, already turning off the main road in their direction.

The two policemen were impassive, swift and businesslike. Doran knew neither of them and longed for the familiar face of Sam, to absolve her and Rodney from the ridiculous feeling of guilt, standing there with a corpse between them, like people in films, discovered still holding a smoking pistol.

While the sergeant examined the body, the constable took statements from them. The two ambulancemen looked on. It was difficult to make statements sound convincing, or even, as Rodney said afterwards, even likely. Yes, they had been taking a walk, in the rain, with

65

no particular goal in mind. They had come across the body in the course of it.

'You didn't move her, sir?'

Rodney braced himself for disapproval. He might not be wearing his dog collar, but felt compelled to behave as if he were, in support of his authenticity in this policeman's eyes.

'As a matter of fact I did, slightly. I know it was wrong, but we had to make sure she was dead.'

Not true. We had to uphold her dignity in death.

'It *was* wrong, sir,' said the sergeant, who had overheard. 'You should never do that. Throws everything out for us. Show me how she was lying when you found her.'

Under the law's two disapproving pairs of eyes, Rodney gently eased Ophelia into something like her original position. By now another police car had arrived, bringing a doctor and a photographer. Rodney and Doran stood back while photographs and measurements were taken and the doctor did his work. It was a long time before at last a body bag was brought, and what had lain on the riverside was professionally packaged into a neat, bundled-up shiny parcel.

' "She that was a woman, sir, but, rest her soul, she's dead",' Rodney quoted, not so low that the sergeant's ear didn't catch it. He viewed Rodney with a cold stare. Said he's a parson. Doesn't look like one. An interferer, shifting the body around like that. His wife looking scared out of her skull. Tempting to tell her she looked as if she'd seen a ghost. She'd probably say perhaps she had. He didn't bother with that old chestnut. He dis- missed them, telling them they would be visited at home for more detailed questioning.

'We weren't body-finders, in his eyes,' Doran said as they tramped back. 'We're suspects. He didn't believe a word we said.'

66

'It's his job not to, until he has proof.'

'Possibly. But he could at least be doubtful without actually taking us for a pair of wandering tinkers with homicidal tendencies. And there was something very curious – he didn't mention her being in fancy dress.'

Rodney pondered. 'Nor he did. Possibly because on his patch everyone goes round in fancy dress. Eastgate, you know.'

'Dealers? Actors from the theatre? Punks? People who buy clothes from Meg? Meg, yes. She's got just about all the antique styles on her racks, mixed in amongst the tat.' Doran was thinking aloud. 'Could that Ophelia dress be one of hers? No. It was made, run up on someone's machine, with those strips of cabochons tacked on. But it might be worth finding out.'

But Meg, disturbed by the telephone from her Sunday afternoon doze, told them she had never handled a dress like the one they described. She didn't enquire what had caused them to ask.

The day slowly returned to normal at Bell House, or something like normal. Kit's friend's mother telephoned to say that Kit wanted to stay to watch the Sunday children's TV serial with Stephen, and she would bring him home afterwards. Rodney and Doran revived themselves with a strong brew of tea, and toasted crumpets with the holes filled deliciously with butter. The banked-down fire most uncharacteristically responded to a new dry log. With the curtains drawn to shut out the iron-grey wetness, the walk and the discovery might never have happened.

Over the remains of the Sunday papers they hardly talked, beyond Rodney's remarks on the incomprehensibility of book reviews nowadays, and Doran saying that she would like to go up to town to a matinée of one of the new productions mentioned. Nothing was said of

Lizzie Siddal, and how she managed to leave her canvas on a wall of the Tate Gallery and transfer herself to a distant Kentish valley, to lie, twice dead, in the slow waters of a river that in life she'd never seen.

And yet, it hadn't been Lizzie, only a mock-up. However eerie the mystery seemed to Doran, it was real, not supernatural.

'I'm glad you were there, too,' she said suddenly.

Rodney looked up over his spectacles. He had been absorbed in an in-depth analysis by an American scholar of a hardly known seventeenth-century poet, who, it seemed, had influenced all subsequent verse writing; but he knew instinctively what she meant.

He smiled. 'Yes. You didn't imagine it. I saw it, too. Don't worry. They'll sort it out.'

Doran wasn't totally sure that they would sort it out. When a newspaper report of the finding appeared there was no mention of bizarre dress, or superficial resemblance to a famous painting. From old habit, and a need for reassurance, she telephoned Sam Eastry.

In late spring Sam had suffered something between a mild coronary and a nervous breakdown. It had seriously alarmed Lydia and their children. He had always been a figure of majestic calm, kind and authoritative, to his family as to strangers. As assurance of refuge and strength in time of trouble. To his colleagues on the force he was a bit over-soft with some offenders, not the sort who looked for violence for its own sake, but one who wouldn't flinch if he happened to meet it. A strong man, rich in old virtues.

And then within a day, he was a shaking wreck, pierced by pains he had never known before; the central figure in a nightmare of fears and apprehensions, as though all the crimes and offences he'd ever been involved with had crowded round him, to form a black cage filled with the poison gases of evil and unhappy feelings.

Poor old Sam, his mates said. Gone to pieces. It happened sometimes in that job. He should never have transferred to HQ and gone for promotion. Too late, at fifty, but he'd wanted it for his family's sake. Eastgate was a rough spot now; a lot of crime, some of it nasty.

Panic attack, the doctor had said. The hospital tests showed nothing else, the psychiatrist found nothing interesting. Just another middle-aged man, suffering from workstress, physical and mental. A fortnight in a rest home would do the trick.

As it had, courtesy of the police welfare services. The house was Georgian, not by the sea, which to Sam represented trouble in one form or another, nor even in Kent, but north of London, in a Hertfordshire village saved from traffic by a bypass, with gardens, an orchard, and a stable of riding-school horses.

There Sam stayed, seeing nobody but those who looked after him, until Lydia and Jennifer visited at weekends. Lydia was equable and cheerful.

'It's been very nasty, but it was meant to be like this, *I* think. You couldn't have gone on as you were, now could you? You'll be as right as rain by the end of next week, you'll see, and we'll manage fine on your pension, now that Jennifer's at school and I can go out to work. I thought we might move back to Abbotsbourne. You can take over a bit of farmland and do something with it, whatever you want. People will like it, having you back, now there's no community cop. Just having you there again will make them feel safe.'

Sam nodded. He was much calmer, now that the nightmare was fading. If Lydia, out of her northern common sense, said things would be best so, then they would be. Through the window of the general sitting room, impersonal yet cosy, he could see the horses' field, and Jennifer in ecstasy over a new foal. Horse-mad, at the My Little Pony stage, was Jennifer. Perhaps he could use the farmland to make her a paddock, and get her a pony of her own. Though there were the roads to think about . . . He stopped himself imagining, as he had been told to, aware that his thoughts were sliding into nightmare country again.

It was Lydia who found the Abbotsbourne cottage, and bought it privately, without using Dixter & Wylie, whom she'd always regarded as twisters, particularly that Rupert. Ben, their son, had an unemployed friend whose looks were unpromising (a pigtail, designer stubble, a premature beer gut), but whose building skills were considerable. He repaired the cottage for them from what Dixter & Wylie would have called 'in need of some modernization' to a state of 'ready to move into'.

He also built a stable for the amiable but less than classically built pony whose arrival transported Jennifer to a little girl's heaven.

'People will like it, having you back . . .' Sam smiled to himself as he listened to Doran, hesitantly telling him over the telephone of her haunting by Lizzie Siddal, and her corpse's seeming materialization in the pool of the Leddon. Doran riding one of her hobbyhorses again. He broke in.

'Doran, it's nice to hear you. All right, are you? Sound a bit tired. Haven't seen you around lately.'

'Oh, I've been about. At the shop a lot – it's difficult without Howell. Sam, I'm sorry to bore you with all this, droning on about Rossetti, but you do understand, don't you? It's so extraordinary about that picture sort of coming to life, only the exact opposite, when we were simply out for a walk. I don't believe it could have been an accident. Only it *must* have been.'

Sam fixed his eyes on a framed photograph of Jennifer as a baby. He was going to be no use to Doran. He knew nothing of Millais, Rossetti or their Ophelia, but made a mental note to look them up in the volumes of the handsome encyclopedia that Lydia had bought as a boxed set to be admired on its shelf.

'Doran, I'm finished with police work,' he said gently. 'I don't want to go chasing any more. The lads who are working on this accident, or suicide, or murder, or whatever it was, will find out all about it. You can bet it'll have nothing to do with you in the end. Just treat it as a nasty experience that's over.'

Just as they had told him about some nasty experiences lurking in his own mind. Though he had nearly forgotten by now, as he was meant to, a hypnotherapist had quietly instructed him to go to sleep, then, even more quietly, ordered him to put out of his consciousness any sights that rose from the past to trouble him. They were over, gone. He no longer had to live with them. He tried, over the telephone, to suggest the same to Doran.

'Yes, I know,' she answered vaguely. 'Rodney said much the same, but I thought I'd tell you, and you might see some factor in it that we can't.'

'I'm not a detective, my dear girl. Just an ex-plod.'

There was silence at the other end. Missing Howell to talk to, he thought.

'Do you remember the Holmes Game?' she asked after a moment. 'When you and I first met I thought police work was all about that sort of thing; nice foggy streets, and gentlemen eating toast, and hearing footsteps on the stairs, heralding yet another interesting client. Oh, what garbage! Now I can't even believe that I believed it.'

'It never was like that,' he told her firmly. 'Except in books. Anything but. And that young girl in the river hadn't been living in one of those sort of stories you used

71

to read. From what you say, she'd been jabbing herself with poisoned needles, destroying her mind. Seeing monsters, having the horrors.' Sam was putting it mildly, but his tone conveyed his feelings. 'Don't get romantic ideas about that girl, Doran. There isn't any way you can help her.'

'Why do they do it, Sam? Young people, with a life ahead?'

'God knows.'

At Doran's end of the telephone he could hear a child laughing. Relieved to be able to change the subject, he said, 'That Kit, is it? Jennifer's enjoying being in the same school as him. Good idea, isn't it, girls growing up alongside boys?'

'Yes.' The tone was curt for Doran, and Sam remembered about the miscarriage. He had to change tack again.

'So you'll forget about this – this corpse?'

'Oh well, I suppose so. It's nothing to do with us, after all.'

Sam put the phone down with the certain knowledge that she would go on worrying, persuade herself that it *was* something to do with her. He knew Doran, and her whims; her tendency to get involved in the dramas which she almost seemed to attract to herself. Some of them had involved him, but not this one. This time it had nothing to do with him. Not even with theories or advice. That belonged to the years when he'd been Abbots-bourne's on-the-spot bobby. Now they hadn't one any more. The authorities had soon got rid of his successor, Glen Lidell, and never replaced him. Economy, no doubt, and, to be honest, there hadn't been all that much to do in Abbotsbourne and district. Still, at times of local trouble, someone who belonged on the spot could reassure people like nobody else could.

Lydia, ironing in the kitchen, had heard her husband

on the telephone, and heard him say Doran's name. Now he was telephoning someone else. She detected a certain changed quality of tone that she recognized. It was how he spoke to old colleagues. She listened this time.

'. . . Can't help taking an interest, as it's my old patch,' he was saying, with an assumed casualness that didn't deceive her. 'Heard anything, have you?'

A long silence followed, broken only by Sam interjecting 'That so?' and 'Mmm'. And finally, 'Yes, well, thanks for telling me. Never know, do you?'

Lydia had put down her iron already. She came straight through to him, and he knew from her expression that he was for it.

'At it again, ringing Jack Grimwade! Yes, I heard you, and I don't mind admitting it. Somebody's got to guard you against yourself. Suppose you have another breakdown – is that what you want? You're not a young man, Sam . . .'

He listened patiently to the tirade, knowing he'd deserved it; not even protesting, hearing her to the end.

'And why you're taking an interest, as you put it, I can't think. Everybody in the village knows by now there was a girl found dead in the river, and that it's nobody from round here, just some wretched junkie from London, probably. They'll tell you all about it at the Rose, or in the shops, yet you have to start asking your pals questions and getting yourself bothered again. Just remember . . .'

'I do remember. It's not like you to henpeck,' Sam said mildly. 'Don't go on, Lyd.'

'Yes, well.' She was calmer now. 'I know it was Doran started you off. She ought to know better, wandering about falling over bodies. Hasn't enough to do, that young woman. Shouldn't have to keep Vi working there all those hours, while she loses money on that shop.'

Sam agreed, for the sake of peace, though he privately thought that Doran had only too much to do. He wouldn't be rash enough to let Lydia catch him making any more enquiries. Indeed, he probably wouldn't make any more, now that he knew that as well as the many puncture marks witnessing the dead girl's condition, a contusion on the neck had been found that suggested a blow which might have caused her actual death. A rabbit punch, to finish off a struggling rabbit . . . ?

The Christmas Sale at St Crispin's church hall was much the same as usual. There was over a month still to go until Christmas, but the festival was an essential in the life of the village, with its offerings of tree ornaments, garlands of bunting and large tinsel stars, home-made produce, and presents which few would wish to receive. Doran found it partly jolly, partly wearisome in its relentless pointing up of all she would have to face in the near future: the decoration of Rodney's church, St Leonard's at Elvesham, the tree, presents on it for all the village children; trailing out there, whatever the weather, to extra services. Not to mention personal Christmas cards and stocking up the fridge for a four-day holiday.

She shook herself out of thoughts unworthy of a clergyman's wife, and indeed of any wife and mother. All these things should have been a joy, not a burden. They had been once, surely, until this cloud or miasma or whatever it was enveloped her. It seemed to have changed her. She was being unfair to Rodney, to everyone.

Enough of it. She paused by the stall that sold eatables. Luscious cakes, pies and biscuits, all but hot from the oven and the hands of the virtuous ladies who beamed, ready and willing to sell, even to disburse change if one gave them a banknote, which seemed to be all one ever had for the smallest purchases.

74

'Ah – your menfolk aren't going to go hungry over Christmas, I see!'

The loud, hearty greeting came from Doran's next-door neighbour. Mrs Louise Kinchen resembled a grey squirrel – thin, alert, quick-moving, bright-eyed, even sharp-toothed, with small claw-like hands and a permanent flush on her cheekbones, like the red tinge of a squirrel's fur in winter. Behind her was her doctor husband, taking a rare afternoon off. Semi-retired, he carried the marks of his years of doctoring in facial lines and wrinkles, furrows of worry about his patients. One of the old school of caring family practitioners: a rare survival, a dinosaur. Doran thought him one of the kindest men she had ever met, well matched by his wife, trying though her unsparing voice might be when one had a headache. Magnolia House was lucky in its owners this time. It *could* only be better after two sex maniacs and a murderer, but Doran counted herself exceptionally fortunate in her new neighbours.

'My menfolk might well go hungry, but for this place,' she replied, adding a Bakewell tart to her growing collection of goodies. 'I'm simply not a cake hand. I once made one that the recipe said would be unforgettable, and it was. Even the pigs at Burrows' Farm looked sideways at it.'

Louise Kinchen laughed indulgently at this quaint, clever neighbour. Doran was always decrying her domestic ability, yet little Kit was a picture of tidiness, and there were always appetizing smells coming from the Bell House kitchen.

'I can recommend that ginger cake.' Mrs Kinchen pointed to one opulently studded with almonds. 'I made it myself, though I *do* say so. Greg adores it.'

The doctor nodded. 'You look as if you could do with some carbohydrates, Doran. What have you been doing to yourself? Not slimming, I hope?' he added suspiciously.

'Oh, no, no. I never do. I mean, I don't need to.' She glanced down at her wand-slim figure, thinner now than before she'd had Kit. Too many scamped meals at the shop? Now that Howell was in London the Port Arms snacks menu had lost its attraction. That meant fewer glasses of fattening beer, too.

'Well, I dare say Christmas will take care of your figure, my dear.'

The Kinchens moved on. Doran worked her way through the press of people, pausing at what was known, with very little justification, as the Antiques Stall.

It would have been the moment for a hollow laugh, but the ladies running the stall wouldn't have taken that kindly, coming from their local expert. Exhibit A, one repro pottery fairing, representing the usual ugly little couple scrambling into a four-poster, with an inscription bordering on the bawdy; though this one was innocuous enough: Last to Bed blows out the Candle. The price on this frankly fake object was excessive. Doran wasn't going to tell them as much, though. The sale was for a good cause, and if somebody wanted to pay that for it, let them. It was sure to sell, as was the much-mended Coalport sugar bowl, the table lamp with a Capodimonte drunk leaning against it, the Disney china fawn with sweeping eyelashes, and the odd cups and saucers which might have been Clarice Cliff or Susie Cooper, but weren't.

Customers were still pouring into the hall: feeble old parties supporting themselves on sticks and walking frames, stout women in check-patterned coats and fake fur flowerpot toques, modern young Dads carrying babies around their necks in slings, their young wives in knee-high boots. Perhaps they'd buy up the pathetic contents of the toy stall: the worn stuffed creatures, no longer wanted – rabbits, cats, a female hare with long elegant legs and a pink mini dress. Its expression pleaded to Doran, who had a weakness for hares. She impulsively bought it, then added a teddy bear, who also had a spurned look in his dim glass eyes.

Rodney, meeting her at the tea-and-cake stall, stared. 'Kit's a bit ancient for those, isn't he?'

'They aren't for him. I just felt sorry for them.'

'Oh, they're for you.' Rodney could always be relied on to understand inconsequentialities. Kit rose from the floor and a pile of books beneath an adjoining stall. He was clutching one of them.

'Can I have this, Daddy? It's got great pictures in. Brilliant.'

Rodney glanced through it and showed it to Doran.

'*Encyclopedia of Demonology*. I think not.'

'Not at any price. Or no price.' Doran returned the book to the floor.

Kit looked disappointed. 'Oh, but they had wings and tails. I thought they were sort of angels.'

'Quite the opposite,' Rodney said. 'We've plenty of pictures of that lot at home, and they're far from pretty. You stick to angels, lad. Doran – look! An old *Rupert Bear Annual*. You want that, don't you?'

'Rupert! A prize, a prize! Wonderful. Twenty-pence – can't be true. Look, Mandy, here's a pound, another. It's still not enough.'

'That's far too much, Mrs Chelmarsh,' the young woman tending the stall protested. Rodney watched in amused exasperation as his hard-up wife fought to pay an honest price for a sought-after old children's book, resisted equally honestly by young Mandy, who could see only a shabby volume. Rupert Bear, in his checked trousers and short little jacket, with his look of eternal innocence, had passed by before her infant days.

Pleased that Doran was pleased, Rodney smiled his hundredth smile that afternoon, enquired yet again how someone was (or their mother, father or grandparent), tried not to look at the tombola stall, where the Rev Edwin Dutton had not permitted any bottles of alcohol as prizes, and tried even harder not to perceive Edwin Dutton himself, hovering near the door in a baggy Father Christmas costume, smiling falsely. No effort could spare Rodney the strains of 'Silent Night', his unfavourite carol, blaring out from a record player.

'Christmas!' he hissed, in a whisper that carried to Doran alone. 'If it weren't for a certain celebration, I should say, *un*like Dickens, that there's a menace in the very name of Christmas. No, excuse that outburst. Some things bring out the worst in me.'

They managed not to encounter the vicar and made for the door. A small Scout Cub was counting the admission takings and arguing with his sister, who accused him of letting some people in free. Beyond lay escape, but Louise Kinchen had caught up with them, eagerly mouthing against the noise:

'I forgot to ask, did you hear any more about that poor girl?'

'No, nothing. If the police traced her, they didn't tell us.'

And let that be the end of it, she thought as they went on out. At Rodney's suggestion, they had said nothing to the police about the Ophelia costume. It could have been a coincidence, a bizarre death-wish fancy of the girl's, or a sick joke on someone's part. Rodney was anxious that his wife shouldn't be publicly associated with any of these, especially with the Lizzie Siddal connection. His conscience told him that perhaps it had been wrong to keep quite – but it was too late now.

'Oh, by the way,' Louise was saying, 'a whole wodge of post came through our letter box this morning, all addressed to you. Will you come and get it, and have a cup of tea, or shall I drop them in? It's that new postman. I'm sure he doesn't look at names properly.'

Tea at the Kinchens' sometimes meant medical students, who lodged there. They tended to carry anatomical specimens about with them and were quite capable, over the toasted crumpets, of producing gruesome bones and jars containing nameless specimens. Hastily, Doran said she had promised to watch a programme with Kit, and confined herself to collecting the mail. She always felt restless when there was no post at all. There had been none that morning, and now she was annoyed to hear that it was lying at the Kinchens', who might at least have dropped it in next door. It proved to be the predictable assortment: Christmas cards, bills, a bank statement, and circulars. There was one letter, though.

Rodney saw her colour change, as it easily did, from that of excitement to shock. She read the letter again, before handing it to him. He scanned the engraved heading.

'The Mill House, Whitbury. Elegant. Do we know the miller?'

'He isn't a miller. He's a collector, he says. Read it.'

The letter informed Box No. PHY, *Barminster Courier*, that the sender thought he or she might be interested to know of a somewhat rare item he had come across recently. It had not yet been offered on the open market. It was in good condition. He was the box number's faithfully, Ralph Janner.

'I advertised,' Doran confessed.

'So I gather. What for?'

The blush deepened. 'Well, Pre-Raphaelite items.'

79

Rodney's disapproval was plain, as she'd known it would be if she'd discussed it before going ahead.

'I see. Any other replies?'

She shook her head. 'I didn't expect any at all. If I'd put an ad in a national arts mag I might have been offered something expensive I couldn't refuse.'

'Like a full-length Burne-Jones of Mary Zambaco as Siren?'

Doran sighed. 'Gorgeous. And stranger things have happened – to other people.'

'Ah, well, our house contents valuation is seventy thousand pounds and we could throw in Kit and Tybalt as make-weights.'

'Those two Burne-Joneses that turned up in a church somewhere fetched nearly a million and a half. I don't see us raising that, even if I hire myself out as an expensive call girl. No, it will be a repro, or a sketch at the most. One of those comic drawings artists were always doing of each other in the odd moment. Some- thing like that. But I've got to go and see it – haven't I?'

The appeal in her eyes was too much for Rodney. He'd hoped that her Pre-Raphaelite infatuation was over, finished off by their tragic find in the pool of the Leddon. But at least the promise of its revival had brought back her old sparkle, and that cheered him.

'Of course.' But he was still wary. 'Want me to come with you? Remote mill houses, unknown chaps. Loot from an unknown source, perhaps? How do you know what it's about?'

She gave him a fleeting kiss, on her way to the telephone.

'It'll be as innocent as an apple pie, you'll see.'

CHAPTER SIX

Whitbury was not exactly a remote village, being only a few miles north of Barminster, but, like so many other rural places, it had lost its railway station in the 1960s. The branch line itself had gone, leaving only a bus service, now down to one bus a week, to the hardship and inconvenience of the villagers, also deprived of their post office and general store, and with the future of their small school hanging in the balance.

All that remained to maintain their community life were the pub and the church. Doran looked in at the church, from habit, and found it over-robustly restored, and with no forgotten Burne-Joneses on its walls. Pity.

The Mill House, obviously, would be a natural target for car-borne tourists' cameras; a modest, comely Georgian dwelling, neighboured by the fall of the river into a broad stretch of placid water where ducks swam and dived. She hated being unable to make an offering to any wild thing that caught her eye, and resolved to ask the man she had come to visit to give her a crust to bestow as she left. That was, if he turned out to be the sort of man one could ask for duck-food on first acquaintance.

When he answered the door, silhouetted against the light from the staircase window overlooking the square hall, she found it difficult to make out his features. She could see that he was tall, sparsely built, dressed in some knee-length robe. Dressing gown? Painter's smock? Overall? Under it was a green velvet jacket, of a slightly old-fashioned cut, and checked trousers. There was a brown beard, shaggy, in that strange style once known as weepers. Whiskers, in fact.

'Do come in,' she heard herself welcomed. 'You're very prompt.' It was the pleasant accent of an educated man, neither young nor old.

'I hate waiting for people,' she told him, 'so I try to be punctual myself.' They stood in the hall for a few moments, exchanging observations about driving conditions and the fine weather for the time of year. Then he led her into another room that felt instantly warm and comfortable. A standard lamp was alight, scarcely necessary in the morning brightness, but giving a cheery touch and helping show off the many interesting objects: pictures on all the walls, a table heaped with books and small decorative pieces. On the mantelpiece above a glowing imitation log fire stood a line-up of figurines.

Instinctively, she moved towards the table, to be stopped, in the politest way, by her host stepping between her and it to draw out a chair for her.

They were sitting opposite one another, his back to the window. She could see Ralph Janner clearly now: unremarkable features, receding dark hair sprinkled with grey, an absence of frown-lines that reassuringly might mean good temper and calm disposition. Wide-open brown eyes, and nice teeth, displayed when he smiled. A blankish face, not much written on it.

He poured from a decanter and passed her a delicately cut glass of dark brown liquid.

'Madeira,' she recognized. 'How stylish.'

He bowed in his chair. 'I think it suits the house better than sherry. Now I find it suits the guest.'

He wanted to please her, it was clear. She was in a mood to be pleased, even flattered. A little familiar of him so soon? Too much butter on the compliment? Never

82

mind. She decided she *would* ask for bread for the ducks when she left.

Emboldened, and enjoying the Madeira's warmth, she was eager to get quickly to the purpose of her visit. A returned compliment offering an opening.

'Has anyone told you,' Doran asked, 'how much like one of the Pre-Raphaelites you look?'

'The balding heads and beards, you mean? Prematurely aged?'

'Oh, I didn't mean that . . . It was just a sort of Burne-Jones impression I had. I've had them on my mind lately, so it probably struck me. But they were such a serious-looking lot, like old gun-dogs.'

'They were Victorians,' he answered, and his manner was quite grave. 'They thought it essential to look serious. Are you a Pre-Raphaelite specialist? The advertisement just said collector.'

'Not an expert, no,' Doran admitted, following dealers' practice of not revealing too much on unknown territory. 'I buy and sell in general. Pictures sometimes, when I like them.' She glanced round the walls. 'And other things. I keep them if our house likes them. It's earlier than this one, and it has very strong fancies of its own. It soon lets me know.'

'What a charming way of putting it. Alas, this isn't my house. I only rent. I had a London one, but . . .' He left the sentence hanging as he swiftly left his chair and went to the table, to return with something wrapped in an embroidered cloth. He laid it on Doran's lap.

'Look at it.'

She unfolded the cloth carefully, making the moment last. What she revealed was a framed picture, roughly a foot long by eight inches broad. It was a drawing, uncoloured, of figures against a background of what looked like tapestry curtains or hangings.

The figures, six of them, were young women in flowing medieval dress, unbelted robes with long full sleeves and rounded necklines. Some were crowned, some wore chaplets or wimples; all looked grave, awed. They seemed to be standing back from two others, a young man, also robed, and a prone female on a bed or bier.

Doran took in the scene at a glance. But one thing alone stood out for her. In the bottom right-hand margin she read: *DGR, May 1852*.

She felt herself freeze with shock. She was aware that Janner was watching her, motionless. She had to say something to recover herself.

'He sometimes wrote his initials as a monogram. Sometimes he signed in full.' Her voice came out strangely, the voice of someone holding a genuine Rossetti drawing on their lap.

'Yes.'

'It's . . . authentic? I mean, have you . . . ?'

'I haven't had it to pieces. The frame and the mount are obviously the originals. But you can see what it is.'

'Can you tell me where you got it?'

He smiled. 'Does one ever reveal a source?'

Now that was interesting. Dealers were always reluctant to reveal sources. Naïve members of the public and even serious collectors were apt to give one a full history of their finds.

'But you're not a dealer, are you?'

He shrugged. 'Not professionally, no. I buy things I like, and pass them on when I've looked at them enough.'

'And . . . you're prepared to pass this on?'

There was a small pause before he said, 'At a price.'

'May I know the price?' She was maintaining her dealer's calm, but it was a tense moment.

His answer did nothing to relieve it. 'One can't help knowing what the last Rossetti painting fetched at auction. It made a headline in my paper. As to a drawing, I can't say. But signed by him, and an attractive subject – well . . .'

Doran was glad she hadn't been able to resist bringing her folding magnifying glass, just in case. She examined the drawing closely through it.

'Dante and Beatrice again. Rossetti's obsession. There's the outline of a canopy over her, and he's warning the maidens not to come too near. His arm flung out, warding them off – that's a very Rossettian gesture. She's got flowers in her hair. I don't think this Beatrice is dead. Just asleep, dreaming. He's telling the others not to wake her. Why would he keep them off, if she were dead?'

Janner was smiling, though with just a suggestion of impatience. 'I've no idea. Perhaps she was infectious. And do corpses necessarily look dead?'

'The ones I've seen, yes.'

'You sound as though you'd seen a few.'

'I've quite recent memories of one.' Doran found herself telling him, even mentioning the Ophelia get-up. He was the sort who would know what she was describing.

'How fascinating,' he said. 'Grim, but fascinating. The newspaper reports must have brought you some good publicity – as a dealer.'

'I hadn't thought of that aspect at all,' Doran said sharply. 'Neither I nor my husband wanted that sort of attention. I'm not a West End tycoon, you know – just the wife of a part-time vicar, with a little shop. So whatever price you have in mind, Mr Janner, I'm sure it's one I couldn't offer to pay.'

Disappointment showed in his face, and, she thought, annoyance. Then as though he passed a hand over it, the look was gone.

'You're very frank,' he complimented her. 'To be frank

85

in return, when I read your ad I didn't know whether you would be the sort of person who could pay my sort of price. You might have been a buyer for the Gettys or the Burrell Collection.'

Doran had to smile. 'Hardly.'

He smiled back. 'Do you want to hear the price?'

'Since I've come here . . .'

'Twenty thousand.'

Doran gasped. 'But that's far too much. Compared with what paintings fetch, and this isn't even a very riveting drawing. It's a bit foggy, for one thing. You'd have to come down a good deal from that.'

'Ah, well, you're the expert.'

'Not at all. Anyway, it would still be far more than I could pay.'

He pondered for a moment, while he poured them both another glass of Madeira. Then he said, 'At any rate, you're professional. Suppose I asked you to handle it for me, through your contacts?'

Doran was startled and thrilled together. She said cautiously, 'Not at twenty thousand pounds.'

'The more it fetches, the more commission you'll get.'

'That hadn't escaped me.'

'Then you would try to sell it for me, at a lower figure?'

He held her eyes, and she sensed that he was willing her to take him and his picture on trust. The brown eyes were compelling, almost hypnotic – or was it the warmth of the gas logs, the wine, the alluring, irresistible scent of old books and pot-pourri, and some oriental sort of perfume, which might be air freshener? Doran was torn between the excitement of having a treasure to handle, and a curious inclination to kick her boots off and relax. But her watch told her the morning was nearly gone, and she was impatient to start researching this discovery which had come her way so unexpectedly. Janner had

86

taken it gently from her and was wrapping it in a sheet of the bubbly plastic packing used professionally for fragile objects. She saw that he must have wrapped many things in that way before.

'You'd trust me?' she said. 'For all you know, I might go off with it and be on a plane to Bolivia, or wherever they don't have extradition treaties.'

'So you might. But somehow I don't think you will. After you telephoned, and very charmingly and wisely mentioned your husband before agreeing to come calling on a male stranger alone, I looked you up.'

He gestured towards a book she knew well, an enquire-within of antique dealers in the British Isles.

'I even looked your clergyman husband up, in *Crockford's*,' he surprised her by adding. 'Forgive me, but I had a feeling you were a dealer.'

It was a little disconcerting to be checked on so – and Rodney, too. But she smiled an acknowledgement that he had done only the right thing. 'Now I know what a picture must feel like when they start investigating its provenance. The way this one's going to feel, in fact.'

'Then we have a deal?'

'I'll have to see what I might get, and consult you.'

'Of course. At the usual commission, naturally.'

He pressed her to let him top up her glass, then went slowly round the room with her. Things on the walls which at first glance had looked attractive and interesting proved to be only ordinary 'smalls', as the trade called them. It reassured her, in a way, to know that the treasure he'd happened to come across was something exceptional even to him.

In the hall he helped her on with her coat, very gallantly and skilfully, so that she found her armholes first time, instead of being forced to scrabble for them. With the door already open, he said, 'You know, if I were you I should think about making something out of that body you found. The art angle, you know. If I thought it fascinating, a lot of other people would. It would draw attention to you – and to that.' His eyes indicated the wrapped picture that she held.

'To this? Another Dead Damozel? I still don't think this one's a Dead Damozel. The Dreaming Damozel, more like.'

He held her car door.

'A Rossettian enough title for anyone. I'm sure we'll do well between us. Goodbye, and good luck.'

Driving off, she realized she had after all not asked for bread for the ducks.

Back at home, Doran had the house to herself. Kit was at school until three, Rodney had gone over to Elvesham. In the old, Carolean part at the back was the room she had fitted out for keeping temporarily things that she wanted to examine for detail or damage, and perhaps restore. It had good natural lighting, and an adjustable standard lamp with a strong bulb.

The longcase clock, which she was now finishing off at home, looked benignly on as she prepared to indulge herself in that ultimate luxury of unwrapping and examining a real 'find'. Tenderly she removed the wrapping. The picture, laid on a table, looked smaller than it had at the Mill House. It was no less exciting, though. The maidens, presumably Beatrice's attendants, in a huddle like scared birds, all had the same face, it seemed, the inexpressive mild features that could have represented anyone. Dante Gabriel probably made them all up if one of his models wasn't around the house. The figure of the other Dante was slightly out of proportion. That didn't worry her. She knew that the early Pre-Raphaelites had not been the greatest draughtsmen, tending to draw over-large heads and short legs. Dante's head, in an extremely unbecoming cap like the ones hairdressing salons used during a perm, was distinctly top-heavy.

But Beatrice was proportionate, obviously drawn from the living model. Lying flat on a raised couch, she presented in half profile the very recognizable features of Lizzie Siddal, pure and perfect, the heavy-lidded eyes closed in repose, not death, the beautiful mouth, short in the upper lip, relaxed, and the long flowing hair straight, not crimped.

Two hardly visible forms – faded perhaps? – held the ends of an equally shadowy canopy over Beatrice. Something stirred in Doran's mind – another picture, very like this. She went to look in Rodney's books, and soon found it. *Dante's Dream*. Thank heaven, it was not the same, though reminiscent: Beatrice lay in the same attitude, but this time the couch *was* her bier; and she was Janey Morris, not Lizzie, with that lady's curving goitrous throat and iron-crinkled tresses. An angel was stooping to kiss her, bending underneath the canopy in an attitude which must have been awkward for its wings.

Doran breathed a sigh of relief. What she had was not a mere copy of *Dante's Dream*, but a sketch for a much earlier scene on the same lines. Beatrice discovered asleep, so Dante warns everybody present not to waken her. Rossetti may not have followed the sketch up with a painting, but that was often the case with most artists. Never mind; the sketch was signed, dated, and important. It would fetch a lot of money. Perhaps Ralph Janner's asking figure. Perhaps even more – or rather less; but still a lot.

Rodney had acquired reading spectacles, quite different in strength and appearance from his distance ones. He said his sight had changed, so that he now needed some specially for close work, but Doran knew it gave him pleasure to put on the new, very large and fashionable octagonal frames, and at once feel younger and trendier. She thought they made him look less academic and also less sexy, but though she pointed this out he replied that he was tired of being a look-alike of Harold Lloyd.

The flashy new spectacles took in the drawing.

'What are they all doing?' their owner asked. 'She could tell from his tone that he was in ultra-critical mood, the kind which usually came on after a parish meeting at which the Reverend Edwin Dutton had been present.

She explained her theory. He wasn't prepared to be easily convinced.

'Why doesn't he want her woken up? Is she having bad nights, and he sees that she's just dropped off, and is telling the others in case they hadn't noticed?'

'How do *I* know? I expect he was about to sneak in a quick . . . chaste embrace.'

'A trifle over-possessive.'

'Oh, Rodney, don't carp. It's a wonderful sketch and I'm incredibly lucky to have been given it to sell. Don't you like it, or something?'

'Mm. A trifle foggy round the edges, isn't it?'

'Not too foggy to hide the signature.'

'And that's what matters most?'

'You know it is.'

'I also know signatures can be faked. Put on years afterwards.'

'You *don't* like it,' Doran accused. 'You're trying to put me off it. What's the matter, really?'

Rodney leaned back against the fireplace, his arms folded, his expression that of one about to say something unpopular.

'I don't like it particularly, though it seems no worse

than a lot of Rossetti's vapid sub-medieval stuff. I can't accept that Dante, who gets hooked on a girl at the age of nine, calmly watches her marry somebody else, then spends the years after her death having angelic visions about her. No, what really worries me is the coincidence about all this. You come across what may or may not be a Rossetti painting at a tacky sale; *we* come across a body dressed like Rossetti's wife-model; then you strike this alleged drawing by him. Who is this chap Janner? If he's so sure the thing's genuine, why hasn't he taken it to a specialist dealer to sell? Why you?'

'He didn't know it was going to be me – me in particular.'

'Didn't he? I wonder. You got home in a very exalted state from that meeting.'

Doran flared. 'If you're implying that I was high, I wasn't. I'd had exactly two glasses of Madeira – of all the respectable, elderly wines.'

'Two too many when you're driving, these days. And you know how alcohol affects you when you're excited.'

'What a suggestion! Would I have driven if I'd had the slightest doubt about myself?'

Rodney knew it would be going too far to ask what her alternative would have been then – to stay over at the Mill House, perhaps? He said nothing. The atmosphere hummed. All too guiltily, Doran remembered the scented warmth of that room, the keen sharpness of the air outside, her own elation, which she knew from experience heightened the effect of even a glass of innocuous cider quite disproportionately. She remembered all too clearly several occasions when she had been stimulated into saying or doing something unwise. And she hadn't quite told him the truth – she *had* had a little more than just the two drinks, and she *had* felt that familiar euphoria starting to creep over her.

She conceded, handsomely she thought, 'All right. I was wrong to have a drink at all, and I suppose it did affect me a bit. But that doesn't alter the details of the drawing, or the fact that I believe in it. I'll take it up to town tomorrow.'

'Bartleby's?'

'No. To someone I know in Bond Street. In fact, I'll take the oil up as well.'

The shop was not hard to find. A single painting dominated its window; an enormous glossy brown horse with a high-arched neck, reins held by a small groom, conscious of his inferiority as a mere human.

There was nothing inferior about Sacheverell Isaac of Bond Street. He was a legend in the world of art dealing. Doran was lucky to know him personally at all, and wouldn't have done if they had not met when he was the official opener of an antiques fair at Barminster. She had talked with him afterwards, and they had got on instantly.

He was elderly, small, neat as a cat, with a soft, accented voice and short-sighted eyes behind heavy spectacles. He had been only a boy when his family had fled from Vienna and the Nazis, but he had seen enough dreadfulness already to be irresistibly turned towards a life among beautiful things. His natural taste and business sense had raised him to a high place of luxury and wealth; but he had stayed inwardly the child who remembered Leopoldstadt, and was never going to forget being afraid.

'I didn't expect for a moment that you'd be free to see me,' Doran said, accepting the super-comfortable chair in what was more a salon than a room behind his gallery where a fantastically elegant black woman was dealing with the ambassador of a foreign millionaire.

'It's a pleasure for me, Doran. And there is not much doing this morning. You bring country air with you.'

'It must be powerful to have got past Charing Cross. Is that really a Stubbs in your window?'

'Would it have been there, otherwise?'

'I suppose not. Which brings me to this.' She opened her huge, soft-leather shoulder carrying bag, which could hold an infinite amount. The drawing was even more securely packed than when it had left the Mill House. Tenderly, with nervous fingers, she unwrapped it and placed it on a viewing easel.

Sacheverell Isaac dimmed one light and boosted others, then repositioned the drawing under them. He produced a loupe, which Doran guessed would be more powerful than any she had ever looked through. Hardly daring to breathe, she watched him survey the drawing from top to bottom, corner to corner. A terrible temptation to chatter almost overcame her, but she forced it back.

'I shall have to remove it from the frame, you realize,' he said at last.

'Yes, of course. I didn't want to risk doing it myself.'

'Quite right.' He spoke softly into a little desk microphone, and the acolyte from the gallery melted in. Melt was the word, Doran thought; she was like dark chocolate, immaculately moulded for catwalk display, with an impossibly small waist, and legs improbably long and shapely. Without speaking, she laid before Sacheverell a pair of gloves, tweezers, and a flat knife blade, before silently vanishing.

Doran watched tensely as the obviously old brown paper backing was expertly slit along the sides of the frame. It had been glued to a piece of board exactly fitting the aperture and secured on each side with small, rusty, headless tacks. They were hard to remove, as she knew,

93

but one by one they yielded. Sacheverell rushed nothing, but seemed to have all the time in the world to concentrate if necessary. Off came the board, and was laid aside. Beneath it were three sheets of rice paper, yellowed with time, cut to the size of the drawing, which at last he removed with infinite care from the cardboard mount, and laid gently on a cloth-spread table.

In the pause, Doran heard him draw a sharp breath. Then he looked at her, and very slightly shook his head.

'Oh no!' she gasped. 'It isn't right?'

'It isn't right, my dear.' His eyes were sad, apologetic for his having to give her the news.

'But – the frame, the paper, that kind of mount – they're a century old. They even smell like it from here.'

'Yes, they do. They are. Rather older, in fact. Rossetti may even have handled them, if it is any comfort to you. But alas, this isn't even a drawing. It's a photograph.'

'A photograph! Not a . . . ?'

'A Hollyertype. You know of them?'

'I'd read something. But . . .'

'Clever old Frederick Hollyer, of Pembroke Square, Kensington. He discovered how to photograph drawings so that they could be reproduced in quantities as originals. The sales added to the artists' profits, while Hollyer earned himself a nice plump living.'

'You mean . . . they cooperated with him?'

'Watts, Burne-Jones, Rossetti. They all cooperated willingly. Don't look so stricken, my dear. Even people like me are taken in, until we learn to recognize the signs. It has been so for more than a century. Look, round the edges, now the mount is removed. The picture fades away – there, and there. And those two greyish patches. And the little fold-mark here, that was on the original paper. This paper has never been folded itself. A wonderful process, this platinotype, and costly for those days, using

94

platinum salts. But, stripped down, there is no mistaking it for what it is.'

Doran could see it all. She nodded miserably. 'Rodney said it looked foggy. I should have known, I should have known.'

'You would have been extremely clever to know, without looking so carefully.' He gave her a concerned look. 'You haven't, by any chance, *bought* this – as a genuine Rossetti?'

'No, thank God. Not that I could have done, anyway. But I was going to get commission, and it would have been lovely to have had that, plus having done what I wanted – found a Pre-Raphaelite.'

He said, very quietly, 'Selina', and the acolyte appeared as softly as smoke.

'I think we might have coffee. Won't you join us? But first, look at this.'

Selina bent her head, a black chrysanthemum, over the table, then shook it sadly.

'We had one a few months ago,' she told Doran. 'Holman Hunt. The person was very disappointed.'

'I know how they felt. How – how much do these things fetch?'

Selina raised beautifully curved eyebrows at her employer, who shrugged.

'It depends how much the buyer wishes to possess such a curiosity. A hundred. More or less.'

Doran thought that disappointed was hardly the word. The coffee, which Selina produced miraculously from a beautiful but useless-looking bureau, in fact a coffee machine in heavy disguise, was strong enough to revive her fallen spirits a fraction. She burrowed in her shoulder bag again.

'Well, so much for Take One. Take Two is this, picked up at a junk sale. Any hope at all?'

Sacheverell scrutinized the oil painting as slowly and thoroughly as he had the other. Beckoning Selina to come and look again, he carried the canvas to a wall mirror and studied its reflection in it. Then he laid it down again.

'Charming,' he said. 'And in the style of, certainly. A slice-up, of course. My guess would be that Rossetti – if it was he – painted the figure and then became bored over the background, as he so often did. I should think there was never much more than this to the canvas, unless one other figure is missing. It could be a study for Rosalind, whom he never did paint, or for the Julia of Hunt's *Proteus and Valentine*. Both used Miss Siddal as their model. Or it could be a copy, or by one of Rossetti's pupils. I simply can't say.'

'Then there *is* some hope?'

Sacheverell spread his hands. 'Who can say? Any signature was obviously on the missing part of the canvas. But it's a pretty thing. Thoroughly cleaned, it might make some sort of price, if only as a furnishing item. Will you leave it with me to show to one or two people?'

'Of course.' Doran was relieved that her own judgement, at least, might prove to have been sound. 'Keep it as long as you like. I didn't really feel very optimistic about it, but it started such a chain of curious coincidences.'

'What curious coincidences?'

She told him all about them. The story was still unfinished when the shop door alarm's discreet shrill indicated that someone wanted to come in. Selina melted away to attend to it. Sacheverell listened to the end of Doran's tale; then he rose and went towards the door. The audience was over.

'What you tell me is quite fascinating, Doran,' he said. 'But you know, I think it may have some sinister element in it. Perhaps that is my way of thinking, always looking for dark motives – my wife says I am a too suspicious man. But I think you should tell someone else about this. Someone whose job it is to look into – coincidences – in which unexplained death has figured. You come to me to assess a work of art. That is my expertise. There are experts in all other things, too, and you should go to one.'

He held the street door for her. Bond Street was a teeming river of crawling traffic, hurrying pedestrians and driving rain.

'Be careful how you go,' was his parting advice. 'It's a treacherous world.'

CHAPTER SEVEN

Doran knew that the one thing Rodney wouldn't say would be 'I told you so'.

Nor did he. When she got home, in the late afternoon, he was reading a story to Kit, who sat on his knee, listening raptly. They were in a world of warm Arabian Nights, where huge stars shone close above a city of minarets, through barred windows, on to marbled floors and splashing fountains, silken couches where lay princes and princesses more lovely than Paradise, rivalling one another in beauty. Feeling guilty at breaking the spell of words, Doran joined them.

Kit jumped down and ran to her for his greeting kiss.

'Mummy, you're tired. Isn't she, Daddy? Did you have to work hard in London?'

'Not really, darling. In fact, I've been to a film.'

'What was it? Would I have liked it?'

'No, you wouldn't. I didn't myself. But it was drier in the cinema than outside.'

And a good place to brood on fakes, and deception, and money; and to think of Frederick Hollyer, photographing away in his modest studio in Pembroke Square, Kensington, that would now seem so rich and strange a neighbourhood to him; and of Rossetti, ceremoniously viewing the print of his dreaming Beatrice – perhaps even as it emerged dripping from the bath of developing fluid; and of Lizzie, lying in her vandalized Highgate grave, without the book of poems that had lain hidden amongst her hair . . .

'A poorish day?' enquired Rodney.

'You could say that. I should have come home earlier, but you know what London's like – once you've taken the trouble to get there it seems wasteful to rush back.'

'Didn't the man like your pictures, Mummy?' Kit asked.

'Not much, darling. Well, he didn't think they were worth a lot of money, which is much the same thing.'

'Oh, poor Mum.' Kit's expression was that of a compassionate baby angel, if one's mind happened to be running on Victorian tombs. Doran turned the conversation to more lively matters until his bedtime.

When they were alone Rodney said, 'I've got to go out again, I'm afraid.'

'Oh, no! On a night like this?'

'Mm. Radio Dela – they want an interview with some old gent. Not far away, but I ought to be leaving soon. I'll need another notebook – and my torch isn't working . . . Didn't Isaac like the drawing?'

Doran gave him a breakdown of the events in Bond Street. He whistled, incredulous.

'Foiled, and by a photographer. And you never guessed?'

'I might have done, if I'd had the sense I was born with and I'd de-framed the thing myself. They come up from time to time, and people are convinced they're right. But *you* thought it was a wrong 'un, didn't you? Come on, now.'

'Well, not for the right reasons, though. There was a kind of aura round it – fading platinotype, from what I now hear. But it didn't make me happy, shall we say?'

'I should have taken notice, and not gone rushing up to town with it. You're so often right about good and evil.'

'I don't say I felt *it* was evil. I merely felt a bit of evil around the place since it came here. I still feel it, by the way. Probably the weather. I'd have called it the Dopèd Damozel, the Druggèd Damozel, the Damnèd Damozel. Do you really think Rossetti thought carefully enough about that poem, by the way? Saying that she leaned out from the gold bar of Heaven suggests the alcoholic type of spirit. She had three Guinness in her hand and the vodkas on the bar were seven. By the way, a friend of yours rang and left a number.'

'A friend? What friend?'

'Somebody you met at a party. Female. The name bypassed me.'

'Oh, Ancilla Ireland? I did tell you about her – after the Bartleby bash.'

'That would be it, then. Sorry, got to rush.' He was already lost to her in the confusion of late departure.

The number was a Barminster one, but the voice at the other end was Ancilla's; a soft, breathy contralto that brought back vividly to Doran the night of the London party.

'It's very cheeky of me,' Ancilla said, 'but I've been in Barminster for the day, and I wondered – you said I might come and see your fans. If it wouldn't be a nuisance . . .'

'Of course not. I'd love to see you. I ought to have asked you before, but things get put off from one day to another. Do you know how to get here?'

She gave instructions. The thought of a visitor wasn't altogether welcome, but it would be unkind to say no; and her memories of Miss – Mrs – Ms Ireland were pleasant enough.

Half an hour later the doorbell rang.

'Well, what a phenomenon!' Doran greeted the visitor.

'For once, someone who understands my directions and doesn't get lost.'

'Oh, I've got a highly developed sense of direction. And yours were so clear. I'm glad to be here. It's simply pouring.'

Ancilla shook her aureole of hair free of its scarf, which, Doran noted, was Hermès. Raindrops glistened in it, and on the blonde fur of her coat, which looked like mink but wasn't. Ancilla saw her glance of approval.

'Strictly non-animal. Isn't it nice to wear something luxurious, and not have to feel guilty?'

'Extremely.' Doran hung the coat up respectfully. Its label bore an impressively famous name. 'If women went about these days swathed in furs, the way they do in the old films, they'd be stoned in the street. Or shot.'

'Why not trapped? That's what their furs' real owners got.'

Ancilla was gazing raptly about her.

'What an enchanting house! Like a perfect dolls' house, but furnished by an expert. Well, you are one, of course. That tallboy! And the curtains! Now those I really *do* know about.'

She picked up a handful of the curtaining, dove-coloured silk, hand-embroidered with tiny flowers, and pronounced that it was French, some eighty years old, that it had been surpassingly well preserved and restored, and would cost a small fortune to buy in the present market.

Doran, almost embarrassed, agreed. 'But I could only get this one pair. Come and see the – well, drawing room, I suppose one still calls it.'

Ancilla was like a happy child loose in a toy shop. She praised the comfort of Rodney's wing chair, the velvet softness of Doran's, the Victorian folding screen covered with a patchwork of cut-outs, the candlesticks supported by a miniature Bow shepherd and shepherdess. Then she plumped herself down tactfully in a chair that was neither Doran's nor Rodney's, clasped her hands in an excited, expectant way (there was something appealingly childish about her, Doran thought), and said, 'Now tell me all about everything.'

'The fans? They're upstairs.' Doran was getting up again to lead the way, but Ancilla stopped her.

'No. About yourself. Your experiences in the antiques trade. I'd love to hear.'

Doran found herself giving her guest an increasingly uninhibited account of the room's contents, how she had come by them, her work, her life, her views on a range of subjects. It was only the clock's striking that brought her back to realization. She jumped up.

'Good heavens! I seem to have been talking for months. I haven't even offered you a drink, or something to eat. How boring. Do forgive me.'

But Ancilla was waving her back into her chair, looking the reverse of feeling bored. Doran fleetingly recalled Browning's 'Porphyria's Lover', and how 'once again laughed the blue eyes without a stain'. Ancilla's wide eyes, bright with intelligence, were smiling like that now. Doran had felt tired and drained after her frustrating day in London; now she felt energy and enthusiasm flowing back into her.

'Bored?' Ancilla was saying. 'I'm totally fascinated. Do you know, you're empathetic. If there is such a word. Yes, there is.'

She settled for a sandwich and a Perrier, while Doran finished the end of a bottle of white wine. Something – stimulation, a change of company? – had given her an appetite for the mound of sandwiches she found she had made. The disappointment of her meeting with

Sacheverell Isaac was receding fast. She didn't even think about the Rossettis.

The two of them sat, talked, ate silently. Only very exceptional guests could be silent in one's company without embarrassment. The house was quiet, Kit unroused by the new voice downstairs, Tybalt invisible. Doran thought fancifully that the house itself was purring gently, as a sleeping cat does when stroked.

With difficulty she persuaded Ancilla to talk about herself. She was thirty-nine. She didn't say whether she was married, and Doran didn't ask. Ancilla said she had worked in various European and American firms, before breaking away and setting up as a freelance consultant on antique textiles to auction houses in both continents.

'Where did you like best?' Doran asked.

'Geneva. I think because it's so clean, sparkling clean, and people are efficient and civil. The lovely Old Town, where I lived, and the new town, looking over that heavenly lake. And I loved the banks.'

'Banks? Of the lake?'

Ancilla laughed. 'No. Money banks. As in manager, and overdraft. I know it sounds peculiar, but I found them – well, so solid. Reassuring. It was like being enclosed by great protective fortresses. Fortresses of wealth. If you felt the world was slipping, you could go into one and sit down, and it came over you like a great comforting cloud.'

It was an odd notion, but Doran thought she grasped it. Money? Respectability? Security? That was most likely it. She could sense that there was some deep insecurity in this sophisticated, cosmopolitan woman's background. A broken home, perhaps? A dayspring mishandled? What was her guest seeing in the glowing fire?

'I loved Zurich, too,' Ancilla said suddenly, smiling.

'It was so balanced. The massive modern commercial buildings, and the medieval part – like one thinks of old Germany, before the bombs.'

'You like things to balance up, don't you?' Doran said. 'Are you a Libran, by any chance?'

'Yes! How clever of you. Not quite typical, though. I'm crossed with Aries, and the Ram often wins over the Scales. Do you believe in astrology, then?'

'Not really. But in some extraordinary way it works.'

They discussed the planets, Doran finding herself embarked on a detailed account of Kit's nativity chart, a thing she dared not talk about to Rodney, who firmly dismissed the science of the stars as pagan.

He would be home soon. For the first time ever she was faintly sorry.

She took Ancilla upstairs to see the fan collection.

'I don't show them much,' she said, lifting three from the long drawer, where they lay in protective wrappings. 'People finger them and start fanning themselves – not very good for the sticks or the fabric.'

'I won't. If you put them on that table I'll just look at them.'

Doran laughed. 'I didn't mean I wouldn't trust *you*. This is the earliest. I know it's seventeenth century, because it came with its pedigree. They were fairly elementary things in those days, and this isn't a great example, but I couldn't resist it because it's so rare.'

Ancilla gazed reverently at the worn handle and shreds of silk and feathers. 'Is it immensely valuable?'

'Not in this condition,' Doran said. 'But another collector might fancy it at a good price, with its bit of paper. This is the one I'm keeping for a rainy day, when I have to sell things off . . .' She unfurled her chief prize, a spread of yellowing lace, glittering all over with tiny gems. 'They're real pearls and diamonds, most of them still there. It was made for very minor royalty, one of the Hanover blue-eyed princesses, and she died young, so they kept her fan out of sentiment. Fortunately for me.'

One by one the fans were revealed, English, French, Chinese, Indian: courtship fans, Presents from Margate, tiny Victorian trifles made to attach to a lady's wrist while she danced, and strong sensible protectors of pale cheeks from the fire's reddening heat. Doran had never had such a silent, awed, appreciative audience for them. It was like showing relics to a devout pilgrim. When she reached the last she asked, not expecting an illuminating reply, 'Which did you like best?'

Ancilla pointed to a small, modest fan of faded silk in a delicate shade of blue. Across the first stick someone had written *Charlotte. 1783.*

Doran gasped. 'How very extraordinary! It's my favourite, too. And I don't know why. It's not specially ornate or even pretty – it just says something to me.'

Ancilla nodded. 'And me. Think what was going on while Charlotte was flirting behind this, somewhere in England. The American War of Independence coming to an end. Mozart and Haydn composing, Reynolds painting, Catherine the Great of Russia being heavy to people. The French Revolution brewing up . . . All sorts.'

'You're omniscient,' Doran congratulated her. 'And I can't think of anyone, except perhaps Rodney, who would think like that. It's almost frightening.'

Ancilla shook her head. 'I'm not omniscient, really, and please don't be frightened of me.' The large blue eyes were full of real pleading. 'I only know properly about a few things that I work in, but a lot of scraps seem to have collected in my brain as well. Thank you for showing me your fans. I feel very privileged. But look, I must go. It's late, and I've got to drive further on.'

'Won't you stay and meet Rodney? He won't be long, and I know he'd enjoy meeting you.'

Ancilla refused, very nicely. Helping her guest on with the luxury fake fur, Doran remembered something.

'Tell me about your name. How is it spelt, and why were you called by it?'

'Well. It's a ridiculous story, really. It's A-N-C-I-L-L-A. It means handmaiden in Latin – hence the k sound for c – and I got it because my mother was frightened by a Pre-Raphaelite. Not exactly frightened, but she got hooked on Victorian paintings, and especially on Rossetti's Annunciation picture, so when I arrived she called me after it. I was just known as Ann for years, of course, but I suddenly thought that was boring and I started using my proper name. I told you it was ridiculous.'

'Not ridiculous,' Doran assured her quickly. 'Fantastic. I know that picture well – the frightened girl crouching on a sort of camp bed, and a very starchy-looking angel holding a madonna lily, as though he were handing her a portable telephone. It's not on my top list, but I can see why it could fascinate someone. Actually, I'm very much into the Pre-Raphaelites myself.' And she was telling Ancilla about things she had vowed to keep to herself in future: the unsigned picture, the discovery of the Ophelia body, the disappointment over the Hollyer. The beautiful eyes grew wider. Ancilla sat down suddenly on the hall chair.

'I can't take this in,' she said. 'I never heard anything so strange. I shall have to mull it over and talk to you again. Oh!'

Something black, soft and heavy landed in her lap, like a jettisoned bomb. It was Tybalt, roused by their voices from his fireside sleep. He weighed twelve pounds, and his claws, which he kept regularly sharpened on trees, began flexing themselves rhythmically in Ancilla's thighs.

'You horrible cat!' Doran fetched him a light tap of admonition. 'I'm so sorry – he doesn't usually do this to strangers. If I pull him off he'll only cling on to you, which is dreadfully painful. You have to unpick the claws . . .'

But Ancilla was smiling down at her torturer, stroking him from head to tail.

'It's all right. I adore cats. It's very flattering to be sat on without an introduction, isn't it? What's your name?'

'He's Tybalt – not Tibbles, as some *will* call him. More than king of cats, from *Romeo and Juliet*, you know. Rodney named him. Oh, your tights – please don't let him do that!'

Ancilla lifted and turned the cat, so that his head was against her shoulder, his eyes blissfully shut, an expression of smug rapture on his face. See how people appreciate me, he was telling Doran. See what a superior, serene cat I am when you're not grudging me the space on one of your senseless books. Now you know how much I deserved that jar of pâté I happened to find in the kitchen. He glinted his eyes briefly, to see whether Doran was properly impressed.

The hall clock struck ten. Ancilla put Tybalt down as though he were made of eggshell china, still caressing him as she did so.

'Tybalt, thank you for your kind attention. Doran, I *must* go. We haven't talked enough. Let's meet again soon – I'll ring you.'

When she had gone Tybalt turned his back on Doran and stalked away without a backward look.

'Thanks from me, too,' she called after him. 'Arrogant beast. But I'm quite glad somebody liked you for a change, besides me.'

Rodney soon came in, tired from the effort of continuous shouted exchanges with the nonagenarian he'd been interviewing, and not anxious for a detailed account of her evening. Which was just as well, since she found herself wanting to luxuriate in the memory of time spent with someone who seemed to have exactly her own tastes and sympathies. We haven't talked enough, her guest had said. It seemed to Doran, looking back, that she'd talked a very great deal – perhaps more than she might have meant to. But she felt warmed, liked, important, stroked, as Tybalt had been.

Sam was feeling superlatively fit. It was a bright sharp morning, his kind of weather. He had slept well. His garden was ruthlessly under control, red berries clustering for the delectation of birds, winter-flowering hebes providing discreet groundcover. Lydia was at the school, where she functioned as a dinner-lady, no doubt happily brewing up another highly superior stew for the kids, more of a Beef Burgundy, she said it was.

Jennifer's pony seemed to be all right, when Sam looked in at the paddock. It was frisking about with a couple of racehorses, in their elegant coats and ankle muffs, and a donkey that a member of one of Doran's animal societies had rescued from some desperate place or other. Brandy, the pony, accepted with signs of gratitude the carrot and apple Sam had brought for him. Sam made a mental note to offer the use of the paddock for any police horses who might be in need of rest and recuperation. Ideal for them.

The church spire reared above the lovely village roofscape, patiently waiting for another Christmas and the joyful voices of the bells. Sam thought of going down there to see that all was well in the belfry; but Rev Dutton kept the church door locked, so that it was necessary to call at the vicarage for the key.

That prospect depressed him. He and Edwin Dutton had met in conflict over several incidents at Eastgate, when the vicar had appeared there in support of various detained people considered by him to be misunderstood, under-privileged members of an uncaring society, and by Sam to be plain cheats and villains. Sam, prompted by some demoniac impulse, had casually cautioned him against bringing prisoners drink or drugs.

'I think you can trust me to do what is best for my friends.' The vicar's smile had been wide, mirthless, and fully expressive of resentment and disapproval of the police as a whole, and this member of it in particular. He was, in Sam's view, the sort of Christian who'd have smiled at the lions when they came roaring out of the traps into the Colosseum arena, and been surprised when they resented it and ate him.

No, he wouldn't go through the rigmarole involved in looking in at St Crispin's. He set off walking homeward, and it was pure chance that as he neared a bus stop the Eastgate bus appeared round the corner of the lane. A reckless idea came to Sam. It was just the sort of day to be at the seaside, to breathe that healthy air, have a look in at Doran's shop, perhaps take a pint at the Port Arms, instead of the pub the police used, which always seemed to be slightly permeated by the cells' aroma of disinfectant and other things.

Without thinking again, he stopped the bus and boarded it.

He had no intention, not the slightest, of seeking out old colleagues on his old patch. He marvelled, as one familiar landmark after another came in view, how feet knew their own way to places, the way cars did when you pointed hem in the right direction. In a bus, you went the way t took you. This one was going towards the Old Town, where the police station just happened to be.

Now that he was no longer subject to the responsibilities and stresses of being on the force, the sight of the building had no power to make his heart sink as it had done in his last months, when it had loomed before him each day like a Temple to Worry. It looked almost bland now, Edwardian bricks and stone dressing gleam- ing cleanly in winter sunshine, official cars neat in their appointed spaces, the usual notices in the usual glazed noticeboard: IF YOU SEE ANYTHING SUSPICIOUS DIAL 999. FIGHT CRIME WITH CARE. DON'T MAKE IT EASY FOR HIM. The usual picture of an old-fashioned burglar with slouch cap, mask, and swag-bag. Funny how that image persisted, when these days they were mostly kids, opportunists . . . His mind shied away from what else some of them were also capable of being. He had been counselled not to let his thoughts dwell on the over-awareness of violence that had led to his breakdown.

His feet knew their way from the bus stop, up the steps, into the hall, across to the front desk.

'Morning all.'

'Can't keep away, then?'

'Just visiting.'

The open plan office beyond the counter was filled with voices and the ringing of telephones – quite different from the peaceful calm he was used to nowadays. Jack Grimwade was obviously tied up in a phone conversation, frowning, scribbling notes, muttering an occasional word into the instrument. Not a good moment. Better leave him to get on with it.

He waited until his friend was at last free; which was how they came shortly to be standing together at the bar of The Case Is Altered, which Sam had promised himself he would avoid. The familiar, slightly sinister odours mingled with that of ale and smoke, troubled him not a all now. In an odd way, they comforted him.

They had talked of his new life, of the benefits o retirement, the pleasures of Abbotsbourne, the joys and anxieties of having children growing up. Jack hadn't beer easy to draw on what was happening in Eastgate at the moment. Talking shop wasn't all that much pleasure when it was that sort of shop, Sam knew. But eventually he worked Jack round to it.

'Any news on that girl in the river, up our way? You had an idea it wasn't straightforward suicide.'

'Had I? Oh, yeah, you rang me. Well, I was right – it wasn't.'

'No?' Sam put down his tankard.

'She was a junkie – had been for months, possibly more, they said. But that wasn't what killed her.'

'The rabbit punch?' Sam asked carefully.

'That's right. X-ray showed the hyoid bone had been fractured. A blow, or strangulation. You specially interested in this case, Sam?'

'Only because it's local, and we don't have many. Hard to break old habits. So, do they know who she was?'

Jack shook his head. 'No traces. Missing Persons have been trying to get a line on her, but you know that isn't easy, with so many drifters nowadays. They're still trying, though – she's been put on ice to give them time.'

Sam's better self told him that what he had been doing was shameless pumping of an ex-colleague. Indefensible. So why had he done it? Old-womanish curiosity, or a hankering for his past profession: a feeling of inadequacy, now that he no longer had an ID card to flash? Or could it just be that Doran had been worried about the dead girl, and he worried about Doran? It would only worry her more to be told about Ophelia, cold in her drawer in the mortuary.

All the same, it didn't stop him going on to the shop to see her. She jumped up as the doorbell clanged.

'Sam! What a lovely surprise. Oh, I've been dreary this morning – alone and palely loitering, as Rodney would say, and I can't go out except for a few minutes because I'm expecting a man from Middleby who might want some of those.' She nodded towards a few pieces of small furniture which stood in a corner, huddling close together like animals in a field, Sam thought. 'Sit down. Talk to me.'

He sat down and talked. It was funny how quickly a casual thing like this, an old friend calling in, could alter her mood, her whole appearance, from wistfulness to bright eagerness, like lighting a lamp. His policeman's eye noted the bareness of the shop, the unattractiveness (to him, anyway) of the scant stock: a dull-looking bookcase bureau, some of those foreign-looking statuettes with a lot of gilt on them, baskets full of cutlery which didn't have the glint of silver from where he was sitting, some pictures and prints of outstanding characterless-ness. Doran saw him eyeing them.

'Seriously boring, aren't they? *I* think so, and I'm ashamed to offer them, but they're all I've got. The cathedral, after Thomas Shepherd, 1829, assorted engravings from nobody knows who, and a portrait of someone's great-grandmother she ought to have sued over. Nothing. Rubbish. I think I'll give it up and go and serve in Patel's supermarket. At least I'd be doing something useful, like selling wrapped sandwiches, which is a public benefaction. And the pay would be regular. What's the matter, Sam? You're wearing your Suppressing Information look.'

Sam said, with a sense of guilt, 'That, er, young woman – the one you and Rodney found in the Leddon.'

As if she were likely to have forgotten.

She was instantly alert. 'Do you know something?'

He already wished he hadn't spoken. 'Nothing substantial.' He outlined briefly what Jack Grimwade had told him, watching its effect on Doran. Her face changed from its brightness to something else: grief? Surely not, for a complete stranger.

'So it was murder?'

'Oh, now.' To himself he sounded like a preposterous character on television, always refuting statements with feebler ones. 'Not necessarily. More likely a blow struck in some kind of struggle. Or a fall.'

'Awkward sort of fall,' Doran replied.

'They've been known. Kids on drugs aren't likely to be conscious what they're doing with their hands, are they?'

'So your people think it was some of them horsing around. She got hit badly, fatally, and they ran off and left her. What's the official title for it?'

'Death in suspicious circumstances.'

'Ah. And what kind of drugs?'

'Hard. Heroin, mostly, by injection.'

'They sit under railway arches,' mused Doran aloud, 'and in doorways, and anywhere else, to shoot themselves up. On river banks, miles from town?'

'You said it – anywhere. What I came to ask you, Doran, was what it was you said about some costume she was dressed in. Ophelia, didn't you say? From Shakespeare?'

'Hamlet's Ophelia, Victorian-style, as painted by John Millais – actually Rossetti's wife, Lizzie Siddal. Just a bit of old curtain lace, in this case. Some fake jewels and a few flowers fastened on – but they *were* fastened on, and she hadn't got herself up on purpose to be found like that, I'll swear.'

'But you haven't told this to the press, or around Abbotsbourne?'

'No, I haven't. You said the CID would know what to do. And Rodney was far from keen on the publicity. He seemed to find it all a bit distasteful, me getting talked about as being mixed up in it in any way.'

Sam scoured his mental reference book and came up with a few images and notes for the cultural instruction of police.

'Some people think that style of painting's very morbid, don't they?' He was recalling his encyclopedia's Lady of Shalott, the dead young poet stretched out on a couch under a London attic window, a white-faced queen recognizing her husband's belt among items a pedlar had picked up on the field of battle, a dead girl floating down a river in a boat . . .

'Yes, they do, Sam,' Doran confirmed. 'Dead morbid. Look, damn the man from Middleby – let's go and have a drink. He can wait half an hour.'

When she got home she said nothing to Rodney about what Sam had told her. It could only make him uneasy on her behalf. Perhaps she would tell him in due course – but she had something else to do that couldn't wait.

She telephoned the number Ralph Janner had given her. It was engaged, then and every time she tried later. She decided impulsively to go back to the Mill House and catch him without warning.

She told Rodney her intention. 'He must be there, simply having interminable phone conversations. Anyway, six o'clock's a good time. People are finished for the day and ready to sit down with a drink.'

Rodney lifted the curtain and glanced out.

'It's a rotten day, absolutely pouring. You don't have to go.'

'I have. I've got to take it back and face him with it. You're here to bed Kit down, so why shouldn't I?'

Rodney longed to say, 'Because I tell you not to.' But in her present mood he knew better than to try to assert himself or argue. 'Just be careful,' he said. 'The roads look slippery and the Barminster traffic's awful at this time. Do you want me to come with you, if I can get young Ellen to come and baby-sit? Then you'd miss the rush hour and we could have a bit of supper at one of the Barminster pubs.' He detested the Barminster pubs, usually packed with tourists, and wanted nothing less than to eat in one on a wet, black winter night. Yes, one thing less – for Doran to be alone and in danger of any kind.

She already had her coat on, its high collar turned up around her scarved head. Her face looked pale, as though the sodium lights of the motorway were already turning it to a livid green-whiteness. He missed the little curls her hair used to twine in. Hyacinth hair, he had called it, borrowing from someone – Milton, even Poe? They seemed to have straightened themselves out, or perhaps she'd flattened them down; and he disliked the effect of whatever rinse she was using on what had been a shining brown.

He pulled her to him, wordlessly offering love, protection, warning. She lifted her mouth to his, and the touch of it was cool, like the outside of a fruit. Only a touch, not the lingering kiss she used to give him when they parted.

He opened the front door for her, then surprised himself by shutting it after her, not wanting to see her drive away. His spirit thoroughly cast down, he went back to the kitchen and the unattractive headlines of the daily paper, still lying where she had left it when she got back from work.

A sudden burst of distant song told him that Kit was still in the bath. He always lingered there if allowed, making the most of the acoustics with whatever song they were learning at school. This evening it was the Pilgrim's Hymn, which Kit knew already because they all loved it. Rodney joined in as he went upstairs:

> 'Hobgoblin nor foul fiend
> Shall daunt his spirit,
> He knows he at the end
> Shall life inherit . . .'

Soaping Kit's shoulders in the bath, he reflected that hobgoblins and foul fiends came in all shapes and sizes, not merely Mephistophelean, and their way of coming into one's life could be either shockingly direct, a bound on to the stage amid fireworks, or a slow ascent through a grave-trap.

He had experienced one of the slow kind at Radio Dela that very morning. After the weekly programme meeting, which Rodney usually enjoyed, Jim Fontenoy, the station manager, had called him into his office. Brightly expectant of a new idea from his mercurial boss, he took the visitors' chair.

Jim began to waffle. It was unlike him, this retelling of old gags, recollections of people who interested Rodney not at all. A faint unease began to touch him.

All the time, Jim had been moving papers on his desk, as though searching for the one that would bring the interview to its point. After going through the file twice, chattering all the while, he gave up the search and fell silent.

'The fact is,' he said at last, in quite a different tone, 'HO have been on to me.' Head Office in London, the All-Powerful, kept a stern watch on its distant outposts.

'Something they don't like?' Rodney knew that it was more often criticism than congratulations.

'Well, yes. At least, it's more of a re-think.'

'Ah.'

'Your spot, you know, going round with your recorder, chatting up old chaps . . . It seems someone's moved down this way to live and seen your jottings in the local rag.'

'And?'

'Thought they were, well, very like your radio bits. Rather too much about old churches, gravestones, epitaphs . . . well, religion.'

'I understood,' Rodney said levelly, 'that I was supposed to be a part-substitute for the old God-spot which got axed, and that it wouldn't be considered actually obscene if I occasionally hinted that I was a parson.'

'Of course. Of course not. That's what made us think it was a great idea you brought us, just when we needed one – what with your knowledge of people and well, your knowledge. Lovely stuff, not too literary for them out there. Trouble is, times change, staff at HO change, ideas change. The thinking now is that we're not offering enough to the young. Music – if you can call it that. A lot more of it, but not direct-personality-identification stuff. Stuff they can listen to without listening, you know?'

Rodney did know. He saw that he was considered to be wasting airtime that someone half his age, with a regional or midatlantic accent, could fill without needing to mention graves, epitaphs, memorial tablets, box-pews, or even the possibility that there might be life after forty. He was being given the push.

Head Office had instructed Jim to apologize and thank

Rodney for all he had done to help Radio Dela establish itself in the county. Jim managed this part enthusiastically, adding his own thanks sincerely and rapidly, with no expectation of Rodney's making any sort of reply or protest. It had been really great, tremendous, brilliant, having had Rodney at his side for so long, always reliable and warm and witty. He was sure that bigger, brighter things beckoned Rodney towards the future, leading him from strength to strength – or at least into the corridor and down in the lift to the street.

He wondered how he would tell Doran. His old car was parked in close proximity to Radio Dela's dustbins. It was almost a candidate for a dustbin itself; and so, he thought as he sat there in it, was he. He had just let himself be deprived, without a cry or struggle, of a nice little monthly cheque which helped to keep the expenses of Bell House paid. He should have argued, reminded Jim of appreciative listeners' calls and letters, asked if there wasn't some other niche for his local knowledge, some new angle he could explore – anything but just let Jim Fontenoy walk all over him.

It wasn't Jim's fault, though; more likely his own, thought Rodney, ever ready to blame himself. He probably had been a bit too churchy, too preoccupied with antiquity and mortality, even a touch morose. Perhaps his broadcasting tone had taken on some of the vocal colour – or lack of it – of the very old people whose memories he'd thought worth preserving on tape. Listeners probably classed him among them: 'That old chap who goes round with his microphone'.

He would tell Doran as soon as she got back from Whitbury. She would be kind about it, but underneath she would be bitterly disappointed. To do this to her, after her letdown by that villain . . .

*

The jangling doorbell, tugged many times, had not been answered, nor the knocker. Ralph Janner was not at home. Doran, weary from the long inanition of traffic jams and the strain of driving after dark against the glare of oncoming headlights, went back to the car and sat wondering what to do.

She had been a fool to ignore Rodney's advice. What a stupid, thoughtless time to drop in on anybody, as if we still lived in a world of cocktails at six. The man was probably gone in London. Or on his way back. Or practically anywhere. Better to go home and write a strong letter tomorrow.

As one last try, she got out of the car and went round the back of the dark, silent house. She had no torch, but could make out a rambling garden and an unevenly paved way to the back door. The house walls streamed with rain. Puddles had formed on the rough ground. Half the door of what looked like a large garage stood open. Doran went in, found a light switch, and was looking at two cars: one small, a modest dark runabout, the other an extra-large estate model, with room for at least four dogs, a day's bag of game, and several passengers.

Or furniture, or carpets, or massive pictures. The kind of car familiar among dealers. Doran pondered on it, tried the handle on the driver's side, and found it locked. The garage contained the usual clutter and two tea chests, which proved to be full of twisted-up newspaper. The newspapers were new, adding to the air of transit about the whole place.

She was back in her own car, just about to start it, when headlights swung round into the drive. An elegant Audi stopped outside the front door. The driver got out and hurried head-bent through the rain, without a glance in the direction where Doran's car stood under trees. He let himself into the house, causing an automatic wave of light from hall to first floor.

After ten minutes, to allow him to settle in, Doran rang the bell again.

Ralph Janner answered the door. He looked annoyed at being disturbed, but appeared not to recognize her.

'Good evening,' Doran said. 'I'm sorry to call without notice.'

'Can I help you?'

'It's me. Doran Fairweather. Chelmarsh. You remember me from the other day?'

He looked surprised, but stepped back to admit her. 'Of course. Do come in.'

The hall was dimmer than she remembered, poorly lit, and the furniture had a secondhand air. But the drawing room was already warm from the simulated logs and rhythmic flames of the gas fire. At a swift glance she took in that there were fewer decorative pieces on the table, and distinctly fewer pictures on the walls. In the air the same fragrance lingered. Her nose also detected a very faint whiff of something like damp hay. Horse gear? Unlikely. He would hardly have been out riding in this weather.

He had moved to take her coat, but she kept it on. He asked her to sit down, but she shook her head when he went to where the decanter stood.

'Well,' he said, sitting opposite her, 'good of you to come so soon. I expect you've some news – about the Rossetti?'

'Yes, I have. I took it up to London, to an expert. It isn't a Rossetti. It isn't a drawing, even. It's a photograph.'

'Photograph!'

'Yes. A contemporary one. By Frederick Hollyer.' She told him briefly about Hollyer. 'I think you could have found some of this out for yourself, before you invited me to make a fool of myself, or worse, showing it round the trade.'

'I knew nothing about it,' he protested. 'I've never heard of Hollyer. I told you, I'm only a collector, an amateur.'

'Not very fair of you to exploit your amateurism amongst professionals, then, is it?' She knew how rude she sounded, but she had been nerving herself up for the interview, and her blood was running hotly. 'I was told that even experts have been deceived by Hollyer, but I do think you should have had this picture investigated before trying to palm it off, and at such a figure. Someone might have parted with cash for it, and then where would they have been? Where would *I* have been when they complained under the Trades Description Act?'

'They wouldn't have got far with that, against a claim of total ignorance.'

'Total ignorance isn't a defence against charges of laying hands on a great deal of money. Nobody fancies being bilked, especially by a dealer – me.'

Janner shrugged. 'You couldn't make out that I was to blame. Trying to do you down. There were no details or claims in my letter.'

True. He'd been careful not to commit himself; but she said, 'If you had the least suspicion that the thing was wrong, you must have known that whoever bought it might show it to an expert, who'd expose it for what it was. Why, when it would certainly be traced back to you?'

Janner smiled. He had a boyish, mischievous smile, which went a certain way to redeeming his slightly saturnine aspect.

'I expect I have a trusting, open disposition, which doesn't look for deceit in others. Just as you didn't –

don't, I suspect. You're really angry with yourself, not with me, aren't you? Or are the police surrounding the house?'

Doran smiled and allowed herself to relax enough to think that his Burne-Jones resemblance wasn't so strong this time.

She admitted, 'I've been dealing for – oh, a good many years, and handling pictures a lot. I ought to have come across a Hollyer by now. Perhaps I've sold one or two on, and never known it. *Caveat emptor.*'

'And perhaps your *emptors* have never found out, either, and are perfectly content with what they got. So – what are you going to do with it? Give me it back? Have you got it with you?'

'It's out in my car. I'll fetch it. I'd like to think you'll make sure it doesn't deceive anyone else, but what you do with it isn't my business any more.'

He had risen as well. 'What an honest person you are. I've heard quite the opposite about a lot of dealers; in fact, I've had experience of some of them. Of course I'll be honest. Now, when you come back in, do take your coat off and have a drink, after that painful discussion.'

'No thanks,' she said from the door. 'I shouldn't have had one last time I was driving, and I simply daren't tonight. But,' she added, having got off her chest what she'd been steeling herself to say, 'a cup of tea would be fine.'

She was soon back with the wrapped picture, which Ralph Janner took and put aside, without examining it. Feeling much more at ease this time, she did take her coat off.

'It occurred to me,' he said, 'that I've got some strictly non-alcoholic red wine. Why didn't I think of it last time? I got it in especially for any visitor who might be driving. Rubbish, of course, from a connoisseur's point of view, or even an ordinary drinker's, but it does taste remotely like real wine, and it's as warming as tea. Like to try it?'

She had had something of the sort before, and gladly accepted a glass. She watched him fill one for himself, and raise it to her.

'To the Muse of Art!' he proposed.

'To Art!' Doran readily agreed. 'We certainly ought to drink to her, when you think how bedevilled she is by bores like Fred Hollyer, not to mention downright fakers.'

As they drank she saw the quizzical way Janner was looking at her.

'You're a very erudite young lady, aren't you?'

'You ought to meet my husband if you think *I'm* erudite.'

'And a very physical one, too,' he added.

'Me? Now that's the last thing I'd say about myself.'

'Oh, it's true. When you first came into this room you looked like a waif off the streets.'

She was going to riposte that that sounded like a back-handed compliment, but she stopped herself. This sort of conversation wasn't one to pursue.

He had refilled her glass without asking. She didn't enjoy the second as much. It was as though the bloom had gone off the fruit, and wine – perhaps even the non-alcoholic type – had seductive qualities. Silenus, rather than young Bacchus, regarded her over the brim of his own glass.

She put her glass down unfinished. 'I must go,' she said, and got her coat. 'Thank you – and watch out for Hollyers next time.'

She thought, as she started the car, that her precipitate departure had really disappointed him.

CHAPTER EIGHT

Doctor Kinchen stood back from Doran's bedside.

'I think she'll do now,' he told Rodney. 'Give her two of these every four hours. Don't let her get up too soon, and keep her quiet. She's had a nasty shock.'

'I will, don't worry, I'll fetch Vi over early, and we'll look after her between us. Any food?'

'Anything light she fancies. Plenty to drink. What she needs is a good sleep. The stuff I've left ought to give her that.'

'Good. Thanks, Greg. I'm sorry about calling you out at such a cruel hour, when Doran isn't even your patient, but the Centre's emergency doctor was out on a call, and she wouldn't let me take her to hospital . . .'

'I know, I know.' As indeed Greg Kinchen did, having been told so more than once by the distracted Rodney. Without complaint he had come out in his winter dressing gown and fur slippers, to find a distressed and battered patient. She had badly sprained her left wrist. Her face and hands were scratched and cut, but otherwise she had emerged mercifully whole from the car crash.

Now the wrist was bandaged, the abrasions cleaned up. She was in bed in their own bedroom, aching all over, her head feeling as though it had been rammed by a pile-driver.

She shut her eyes. The events of earlier that evening came flooding back: the warmth and the wine, and something else only realized when she was back on the road again and finding her vision oddly blurred, doubling and trebling the oncoming headlights.

The after-taste of the wine was faintly chemical. She had sampled non-alcoholic drinks before, but none with such a curious flavour; not one that any reputable firm would count on to sell its product.

And the blend of scents in that room. It came to her now, after breathing fresh air. The top-note in them had been something like damp hay.

Dope, of course, she realized. Howell's cottage and his car interior sometimes smelt like that. How dim of her not to have recognized it at once. It wouldn't have made her get up and leave the Mill House hastily if she had: people did take the stuff, and it didn't necessarily signify villainy. But what had been in her drink had been something else — what, and why? Had Ralph Janner intended to seduce her? What else? Surely not rob her?

It all seemed most unlikely. And why should he keep spiked drink ready? He hadn't been expecting her to call, so it couldn't have been for her express benefit. But then she remembered the few minutes when she'd left him alone while she went back to her car for the picture. That was his chance, if there was any truth in it.

What a fool to accept drink at all, especially since Rodney had been critical about last time. Well, at least she'd felt competent to drive. Not competent enough, evidently, she realized with a pang of terror. Halfway to Barminster a gigantic transport's powerful headlights had come swooping down on her, blinding her. She swerved wildly, in panic. Her hands came off the wheel, and a shocking impact smashed the car to a halt.

For moments, everything was quiet. Then she heard the truck driver's language. It was explicit, squarely blaming everything on Doran. She thought he'd had a bad shock, too. When he'd seen that she was all right he went to assess the damage. His own bumper was bent, but it was the tree she'd run off the road into that had stopped her so abruptly. But for her seat belt, the man told her . . .

The police he fetched by telephone said the same. She was very lucky to be alive. Home was nearer than the nearest hospital, which had no casualty department, anyway. She begged them, as coherently as she could manage, to be taken home.

Her last thought, as the doctor's sedative began to work, was that it was no thanks to Ralph Janner that she was alive. Had he had the slightest idea what effect his wine might have on her? Was he what he would have her believe him to be? She fell asleep with the question unresolved.

Rodney was very angry. The anxiety of waiting had stressed his nerves. Then had come the anticlimax of relief when the police telephoned him; and then they had brought her home in pain and shock. He tried not to let his anger spill over on to her, but when the police had gone, and the doctor was awaited, she'd mumbled her suspicions of Janner's wine. Then Rodney's fury knew no limits.

The day after the crash she was calm but dozy, after some more of the doctor's stuff. Rodney could leave her in Vi's care. He got out his own ancient car – hers had been towed from the scene of the accident to a garage, almost a write-off, they'd telephoned to report. He drove over to the Mill House and parked noisily outside the front door.

'Ralph Janner?' he asked the unshaven man who answered the door in his dressing gown, though it was mid-morning.

'Yes. I don't think I know you, do I?'

'My name's Chelmarsh. You *do* know my wife.'

Grim-faced, Rodney was in the house before Janner could protest. He strode straight into the drawing room off the hall, before swinging round on his protesting host.

'My wife came to see you yesterday. She brought your so-called Rossetti picture back. You gave her something to drink that you told her was non-alcoholic. On the way home she lost control of her car and only just escaped being killed.'

Janner looked dazed, shaking his head incredulously.

'I – I'm terribly sorry. I can't imagine why . . .'

'Why did you persuade a woman who was driving to drink?'

'It was non-alcoholic. You just said so yourself. Harmless.'

'I said you *told* her it was. Will you show it to me?'

Janner went to the drinks cupboard and brought out a bottle that had been re-stoppered. Rodney withdrew the device and sniffed. Then he sealed it again.

'I'm going to take this away and have it analysed,' he said.

'For heaven's sake, it's just what it says on the label. No alcohol at all. What is all this?'

'My wife was breathalysed negative. I don't want it tested for alcohol – for drugs.'

A change came over Janner's face. What it was, Rodney could never recall. The eyes, the changing size of their pupils, perhaps; or a darkening flush on the stubbled cheeks. Rodney didn't have time to consider. Calling him things that he'd never been called before, Janner leaped at him, his hands scrabbling for the bottle. Responding in words that he wasn't accustomed to using, Rodney resisted. It was what could only be termed a brawl, both of them twisting and struggling after the wine bottle. Rodney, who had possession, was tempted to use it as a weapon of self-defence. It did occur to him, though, that he'd no right to be on his assailant's premises in the first place. He wasn't the law or its representative. If he knocked Janner over the head he would be in deep trouble for committing an assault, and that wouldn't help Doran at all.

Wresting himself free, and leaving Janner in possession of his bottle, he ran from the room. The front door was still wide open. He slammed it shut behind him. It gave him just enough time to throw himself into his car, start up, and drive off.

'So that was it,' he told Doran. 'I had to give up. It would all be very hard to prove that he gave you drugged wine with evil intent, even if that was the same bottle. He could have put the stuff into your glass – if there was any stuff at all, and he really did mean you harm. We haven't got a case. I disliked the man, I disliked the place, but there's nothing we can do out of pure suspicion.'

Doran was propped up with pillows. With the bandages, and her pale face, Rodney thought how young and vulnerable she appeared.

'You've done enough,' she insisted. 'Thank you, love. Anyway, that's that. I suggest we forget the whole business – apart from the car insurance claim. Just be thankful I don't have to see him any more, and I'm nearly all right now.'

But he knew she was not all right. He talked to Greg Kinchen.

'She's shocked, of course,' the doctor said. 'And she's what might be called a bit low.'

'Low?'

'Nothing serious. But she's obviously underweight. Nervy. Anything on her mind?'

Rodney thought. 'Well, the shop, I suppose. Money, in general. Howell not being about, to help her. And this idiotic Pre-Raphaelite obsession she's had lately. That wretched, morbid lot! I swear they reach out to trap people.'

Greg frowned. 'This isn't like you, Rodney. If I were you, as soon as she's up to it, I'd take her along to that little church of yours and hold a very small service, just for yourselves. And when you come back you'll both feel much better for it.'

Unique advice from a doctor, Rodney thought. But Greg Kinchen had come to know his neighbours well; and when he saw them both together, over Christmas, he was pleased to observe that the prescription had worked.

Christmas came and went, bringing its special workload for both Rodney and Doran. This year she was glad of it. There was escape and relief in organizing events at Elvesham, where Rodney's parishioners outdid themselves to prove that what Abbotsbourne could do, they could do better, even if they only had a service once a month. St Leonard's, its tower propped up by scaffolding, was as cheerful inside as hands could make it. Annabella Firle, now making a living as a commercial artist, had created Christmas tableaux from wood, paper sculpture and an amazing variety of materials. The ladies of the village had been begged to give their odd earrings – 'because everybody's got lots of odd ones' – and foil wrappings off groceries had been transformed into the wings of angels of all sizes. The result, glittering among sheaves of winter greenery, was dazzling, a credit to the parish. Even Edwin Dutton came and admired, though he couldn't refrain from remarking that decorations were a rather unimportant part of community spirit, which could be expressed in more practical and useful ways.

The Chelmarshes' own tree – artificial, because they

didn't hold with the sacrifice of real ones, and hoped Kit would grow up feeling the same – was a glory of vari-coloured tinsels, lights and bright baubles, ranging from new unbreakable ones from the village stationer's to old and beautiful miniature birds with spun-glass tails. Kit was allowed to stroke their backs, because he had been brought up with antiques and could be trusted to respect fragility.

His parents had been fully agreed in excluding Santa Claus from the family circle. He was, as Rodney said, a fraud, and not a pious one, at that.

'When Kit gets taken into Barminster he'll see at least half a dozen Santa Clauses, or Santae Clausi, or whatever, sitting in the stores, handing out rubbish trinkets and breathing beer fumes over credulous children. Or not even credulous, these days. Why prop up what isn't even a legend, just a commercial spin-off from a rather frightful American nineteenth-century poem? If anyone brings him presents, it's us, and friends, and they're really a gesture in honour of the Christ-child. So any human child who gets one had better be good and deserve it. Agreed?'

'Agreed.'

So Kit had been told the truth about Santa from the very first. He accepted it without question, because his parents said it was so; and he soon grew sharp enough to notice that such of his friends as were still into Clausdom had their own reservations about reindeer, and chimney space, and, on many of their homes, absence of chimneys at all.

The only embarrassing outcome had been when he was four, and Doran had taken him to visit Santa's Grotto in Barminster's biggest store because it was said to be remarkably pretty. Kit had gone up to Santa, looked up into the whiskered face, and said, 'I hope you get a part again soon. Couldn't you be in pantomime?' He wondered why everyone laughed, including Santa: because he *had* been told that they were all out-of-work actors . . .

And now all the excitement was over, and the grey face of New Year turned towards them. The bills, which Doran had managed not to think about during the break from the shop, duly rolled in, threatening to engulf her personal bank account. She consulted Howell.

'They say the rates are going up again – over a quarter this time. How am I to go on?'

'Like I told you before – don't. It's a dead loss, the dealing game, unless you're in real big. Chuck it up.'

'I can't. What would I do? Besides, once I let my contacts slip I'd never get them back if things changed.'

'Do the antiques fairs. Peddle stuff around. You'll pick up stock easier that way. They all do.'

Doran knew this was true. But she couldn't contemplate a life of constant travelling about, leaving her family to fend for themselves while she stood about gossiping and drinking mugs of tea with fellow dealers while they waited for the punters to come forward. And yet, something in the prospect appealed to the restlessness in her.

'I think I'm waiting for a sign. You needn't snort, Howell – they do come occasionally, to show one which way to go.'

She found a supporter in Ancilla, who, after a telephone chat that was somewhat melancholy on Doran's part, insisted on coming down to buy her and Rodney lunch at Abbotsbourne's local, the Rose Reviv'd, which she had chanced to see written up somewhere. The Rose had moved very much upmarket under new management, and was now more restaurant than pub, and fairly expensive, with only a very small bar in which non-eaters were not encouraged to linger.

The Chelmarshes rather disliked the Rose in this new form, and scarcely used it, but they found they could suppress their prejudice in the interest of giving Ancilla the pleasure of entertaining them there.

'I call this truly civilized,' she approved. 'The perfect pub for a perfect village. I've only seen it in the dark before, that night I called on you. And you've even got a river. So shy and modest at first, then coming into its own as it goes to join the sea; and always alive . . .'

Meeting Rodney for the first time, she had impressed him with her elegant hound's-tooth check tailored suit, not too power-dressing conscious. It gave the effect of silver from a distance, and set off piquantly her dandelion-clock hair. He had somehow expected not to take to Doran's new friend. From Doran's description, she had sounded the gushing sort.

But here she was, making him feel that *he* was just as much her friend. Far from gushing, she wanted to hear all about him. What drew him into the church in the first place? What had influenced him as a boy? What was his favourite part of England?

He told her all these things, and more. At times, Doran wanted to intervene, 'But you've never told *me* that!' She could see that he approved Ancilla's way of speaking, clear yet not loud. People's voices told him a lot about them.

For Doran, she had words of encouragement: 'Hold on. It will come right again. I had a bad patch like yours once, and I can tell you from experience it doesn't do to let them get you down.'

'*Nil illegitimi* . . .' Rodney murmured.

'Exactly, Rodney. Mind you, Doran, you're too modest for your own good. You've got superb taste, and you need to exploit it.'

133

'But how?'

'Well, for instance, that photograph – Hollyer, wasn't it called? Instead of taking it back to the man who wished it on to you, you ought to have cashed in on it: brought it to public attention, written an article about Fakes and Non-Fakes, or something; made the antiques world sit up and notice you.'

'I suppose so. But after the crash I rather wanted to forget the whole thing.'

'Don't,' Ancilla said earnestly. 'I know you had a nasty shock before, too, when you found that poor girl in the river. But, you see, that could have been good out of bad for you, by giving you publicity, if you'd only let it be known that you recognized the costume from the Burne-Jones painting.'

'Millais,' Doran corrected automatically. 'It's easy to mix them up, but it was Millais painted *Ophelia*. Anyway, I don't want publicity of that sort. Too horrible.'

'Much,' agreed Rodney, who shared Doran's knowledge that it had been murder, and preferred not to discuss it in public, especially over lunch. He turned the conversation to food.

The meal was most pleasant, but Doran caught a glimpse of the bill as Ancilla claimed it, and sympathized with the expression of shock that flitted across her face. At least the old Rose had been cheap, as well as cheerful.

She was touched when Ancilla presented her with a napkin into which she had scooped a generous piece of fish: 'For Tybalt, with my compliments.'

They parted company afterwards. On their way home they discussed their hostess. Rodney said, 'Ancilla, "Behold the handmaid of the Lord". Well, I don't know about that, but personal attendant on the Three Graces, certainly.'

'Are you being catty?'

'Not a bit. She's obviously an amazing lady. I'd forgotten what it felt like to be appreciated – except by you, of course. Did I talk too much? I felt I was doing.'

'Odd,' Doran remembered. 'I felt like that when she came to our house. I'd rather like her to come again and stay. She cheers me up.'

'In that case, she shall.'

Doran left the shop shut for a fortnight after the Christmas holidays. It was a time of year when little or no trade was to be expected, when prosperous dealers took foreign holidays, and poor ones put a card with a home telephone number in the shop window. Doran's card produced just one enquiry, from an elderly winter resident of Eastgate who fancied a nice little trinket box, and was markedly disbelieving when Doran told her that it was badly damaged and not for sale.

'Then you shouldn't have it in the window, should you? I suppose the fact is you don't want the trouble of coming all this way to get it out for me,' she said sharply.

Doran replied that she would have come to the shop with pleasure if the piece had been genuinely saleable, but it wasn't.

Meg Rye was her keyholder and neighbourhood-watcher, living as she did over her secondhand clothes shop just on the corner. But to ask Meg to go in would mean the disturbance of the burglar alarm and the possibility of Meg flapping if she couldn't cope with it. So much for winter trade.

Doran was glad to be off the roads for her extended holiday. Rodney's old banger was not up to the wear and tear of regular journeys, threatening, if over-pressed, to present them with the need for a costly overhaul and unaffordable replacement parts.

'So much for being a "two-car family",' she said.

'Anyway, we aren't any more, till we get the insurance for mine.'

'My MOT's due next month,' he said unhappily. 'They'll never pass the tyres and they're a fortune to replace.'

'Why not let it go?' she suggested. 'I'll have something new by then – well, new-secondhand. We could share it, between Dela and the shop.'

Rodney threw her an even more troubled look. He began to say something, but an instinct she couldn't have explained prompted her to interrupt him. Now that she thought about it, his Radio Dela jobs lately seemed to have been few and far between.

'Anyway, the question doesn't arise yet,' she added quickly, 'I'm quite glad not to have to be in Eastgate at this time of year.'

'Everybody should be glad to be out of Eastgate, or any other English seaside resort, at this time of year,' Rodney replied darkly, ' "Where but to think is to be full of sorrow, and leaden-eyed despair . . ." '

'Oh, I wouldn't go as far as that. You used to say you liked places out of season. You said they were more atmospheric and peaceful.'

'Aye, the peace of the graveyard, as Middleton Murry put it. Or was it someone else?'

Doran sighed. She saw how hard he was trying to get off the subject of money. At this rate, Eastgate was going to seem jollier than Bell House, when she went back to it.

She returned there on a bright, fair morning with a crisp breeze blowing salty air into the narrow street where her shop was. Its window was intact – no damaging evidence of Christmas revellers, though a cluster of lager cans had collected in her doorway, and there were signs that the pedestrian street had been used for other unintended purposes.

Doran studied the window critically. The flawed trinket box was still there; the person who had coveted it had not been driven to crime by the lust to possess. Otherwise, the few bits and pieces on display wouldn't have tempted the most chronic kleptomaniac.

She was determined to treat the place to a change for its reopening; something to perk up the trade's interest in it, before they gave her up as not worth calling on. If she brought from home the Clarice Cliff Bizarre tea set which had been enlivening a kitchen shelf with its jazzy tones, and sacrificed an early plate with a glaring Divine eye and an ominous text, the buyers would be round. Just to cheer up the window she might display one of her fans – though with a prominent Not For Sale label.

Inside, she found nothing sinister through the letter box; a couple of late, hand-delivered Christmas cards, the inevitable two copies of the same issue of a free newspaper, an official brown envelope, a circular advertising a concert which had come and gone. No trade cards – not surprising – but a note from Howell, saying he'd popped over to a nice little spot in Provence for a few days with a friend who was buying a house over there.

Doran switched on the kettle for coffee. The tap-water was the colour of coffee itself until she ran it clear. Rinsing her favourite mug, she glanced up and took down a second mug, seeing the dumpy figure of Meg approaching at speed.

'Good,' Doran greeted her thankfully; 'Just in time. Coffee and a gossip. Oh, and Happy New Year.'

Meg returned the greeting, but her face was lacking its usual beam, and Doran didn't receive her customary 'kiss, kiss' salutation. Meg was an eccentric dresser at any time, but this morning her selection of clothes seemed

even more random, topped by a man's dressing gown
She had a piece of paper in her hand.

'Had one of these?' she gasped. 'No, or you wouldn't
be sitting there so calm. Read it, read it.'

It was a letter and set of forms, bearing the heading of
Eastgate and District Council. In silence but for Meg's
heaving sounds of distress, Doran read it with increasing
alarm.

A figure in bold print made her gasp. She looked at
Meg, who was watching her.

'I don't believe this.'

'We didn't, either, but it's true. Peg rang their offices
and checked.'

'But it's a printing error, surely, this figure?'

Meg shook her head. 'Look at your own.' Her eyes
indicated Doran's unopened brown envelope.

What she found in it struck an icy chill in her. Under
the new rating system for commercial premises she was
going to have to find an extra £3,000 a year to stay in
business.

'But they can't!' she said, as well as her parched mouth
would let her.

'They can. They have,' Meg said, with a kind of
gloomy triumph. 'Everybody's got one. They've socked
it to Peg and me worse than you because we live over the
shop. So much for all this pedestrianizing that they've
wasted their money on. It hasn't brought a ha'porth more
business to any of us – less, now that cars can't get near.
Honestly, I don't know what we're going to do. It's not
as if Peg had another trade in his fingers, except for his
bits of sketches that tourists buy. I can sew and cut out
and design a bit – I went to art school, you know – but
where's a living in that nowadays?'

Abruptly Meg burst into noisy tears, scrabbling among
her assorted robes for a handkerchief which she couldn't

find. Doran handed her a box of tissues and got up, giving Meg's shoulder a little pat. There was nothing else she could do except make the coffee. The kettle had boiled and switched itself off. She spooned the instant brew and put a mug beside Meg, whose gulps and sniffs subsided under its influence.

'Awful,' Doran apologized for the coffee, which looked and tasted like sludge. 'How long does powdered milk keep?'

'We can't go on,' Meg said. 'It's the finish of us.'

'Me too,' Doran said flatly.

Meg looked up in surprise. 'You're all right, aren't you? I mean, there's Rodney – and Howell would find you some connections. Not like Peg and me, with nothing to fall back on.' Her tone dismissed Doran's problems as negligible, compared with hers, as she gabbled on about how Peg and she were going to live, and where, and what it would do to his nerves, and whether she'd be able to shift her stock of secondhand clothes before they had to get out, or finish up giving them away.

Doran interrupted at last. 'Meg, I'm sure you'll manage. This *is* the highest-rated part of town, and you don't need a shop really. Find somewhere to live further out, and rely on the markets and fairs for your things. It'll mean moving about, but that won't do you any harm.'

Nor would it. Meg was as sturdy and spherical as the babushka doll she resembled, while her husband's famous nerves could only benefit from a change of gossiping cronies and drinking companions. But the advice Doran had given echoed that given by Howell on leaving the partnership. She knew how bad all the omens were for herself. The dwindling number of antiques shops would vanish, the premises to be leased briefly by ephemeral boutiques and charity-backed shops, or simply abandoned, with boarded-up windows serving as bill-boards with posters for grotesquely named rock bands. Some day a developer would buy out the survivors, and pull the whole lot down to make way for some such pathetic gesture towards Disneyland as Eastgate Harbour Fun and Leisure Centre.

And it would all end in disreputable decay, as the old pleasure gardens had done: Cremorne, Vauxhall, Rosher-ville – where were they now, the bright lights, the music and masked dancers?

But she wouldn't be there to witness any of this decline. She knew that the rates-explosion effectively blew up the last of her hopes of struggling on with the shop.

Meg had brought a petition of protest that several of the locals had signed already. Doran added her name willingly to the crumpled paper; but she knew it would do no good. Doran Fairweather Antiques was finished.

Rodney listened, not commenting, a thing he was good at. When she had finished, he said, almost as though addressing himself, 'I knew it would happen. All the signs were there.' He sighed and added, 'Well, you'll have to shut up shop. Literally.'

'Yes. Unless I can find an outlet somewhere else – here, perhaps, in the valley. Oh, well, at least I can cut down on Vi. She won't mind, everybody wants her. And we'll still have your stipend for St Leonard's, and the freelance money.'

Rodney turned away, staring out unseeingly over the rainy garden.

'I have to tell you something.' He turned back to face her. 'I've been a coward, not telling you before. I've lost my Dela spot.'

She had wondered once or twice recently what there might be on his mind. She hadn't asked, because if it were some parishioner's trouble that was concerning him he would either share it with her voluntarily, or not at all.

'It happened before Christmas,' he went on. 'Jim Fontenoy asked me to drop into his office. He chatted of this and that, and then, quite lightheartedly but firmly, gave me the boot. You know: "Thanks old chap. Drop in some time, always glad to see you. But out. Nevermore." '

'Oh, darling! But why?'

'My image, I gathered. Too antique, fusty. "You are old, Father Rodney, the young man said, and your hair has become very white, and yet you incessantly stand on your head: do you think, at your age, it is right?" I suppose my mild buffoonery *is* rather dated.'

'My darling, I'm so sorry. The rat! I wouldn't have thought it of Jim. But why didn't you tell me before?'

He shrugged. 'Didn't want to worry you. Thought it would somehow go away by itself. Sheer cowardice. Forgive me?'

'Of course, except for bearing it on your own, you clot.' She knew the hurt he must feel; the rejection, the deprivation of the small things which had filled up the gaps in his once-full life, and made him feel useful and wanted: the interviews, the discoveries, the social contacts with radio people and listeners . . .

'It's been rotten for you,' she said, 'rotten enough without this shop trouble. But now that's going too, we'll have almost nothing coming in, except your stipend.'

Rodney took a deep, preparatory breath.

'Since this is Confession Time, I'd better tell all – I've been considering chucking in my hand there.'

'The church? How?'

'Well, I have to face it, the blasted Alternative Services

141

and the English-for-Retarded-Infants Bible are here to stay. They've moved in, like squatters, and they'll never go away again, however much dinosaurs like me rage and steam. But if I call myself a Christian, can't I accept them for the good thing they must be for somebody: the letter killeth, but the spirit giveth life? Just a case of setting my teeth, apologizing for being stubborn and froward, and . . .'

He broke off. In the long pause Doran quietly asked, 'And?'

'Offer myself for a real administrative parish. Anywhere. With a vicarage thrown in.'

For the second time that day Doran felt the cold grip of shock. She heard her voice tremble.

'So you did?'

'I did. Last week, when the Archbishop was in residence and I knew the rest of the top brass would be there, all primed up to take decisions. A nice, civilized, reasonable Dean talked to me, and listened to me, and then said I could hardly expect another plum rural parish in the South-east to be waiting to drop into my lap, now could I? Or the South-west, come to that. He said it was a tough world out there nowadays, and it was his personal view that I wasn't temperamentally suited to the modern needs of the modern Church.'

Rodney paused again, then resumed. 'However – it's all right, darling, I'm coming to it – there was one parish almost immediately available, if I really thought myself up to the challenge.'

'Where?'

'Wykeworth. Industrial town in the far North-east. A big area to cover, lots of shipyard and mining unemployment, all sorts of problems, and really hard work. *But* a small modern vicarage in a new industrial estate, and quite good money – not to mention a car allowance. I've got a month to make my mind up whether to apply – *our* minds.'

This isn't happening, Doran told herself, as she had often done in moments of crisis or pain. If one detaches one's mind it will all go away like the illusion it is. Real agony only lasts a fraction of time. When the clock ticks on to the next moment the worst will have faded, the words become mere echoes.

She said, 'I'd better get supper started.'

They were very calm during the meal, listening to Kit's account of his school day, discussing trivia. Kit was quiet, too, sensing their mood, not giving them his usual snatches of impersonation or reciting something new he'd learned.

'May I go up early and read?' he asked after not quite finishing his pudding.

'Yes, of course, darling.'

As he kissed Doran good night he asked, 'Nobody's ill, are they?'

Rodney answered, 'No, Kit. Everybody's quite well – thank God.'

When Kit had gone upstairs, he added, 'I wonder if Shakespeare based his little boys on Hamnet?'

'Hamlet?'

'No, Hamnet, his son. He died aged eleven while William was away touring. Where did Mamillius come from, and young Macduff? He'd certainly known some small boy, old before his time and too wise for his years . . .'

'Rodney! I'm not having Kit labelled too-good-to-live. He's just very sensitive. That's one good reason why I'm not really sorry about having to give the shop up. He needs far more of me than he's been getting.'

'I think that's true. And maybe he needs something more in the way of mixing with others than just going to play with Paul and Stephen. Perhaps it would do us good as a family.'

But they weren't ready to talk about Wykeworth yet. Only at bedtime, after an evening of reading and desultory talk, Doran burst out, 'If that wretched Hollyertype had been real, a real Rossetti drawing, none of this would matter. Just my luck to pick a miserable photographic mock-up. What a difference it would have made.'

'Not as much as you think, my love. It wouldn't have kept the shop going for long. And somehow I feel it would have been ill-gotten gold. There was a distinctly nasty aura about Master Janner and his Dreaming Damozel. What sort of sleep was it that Dante didn't want them waking Beatrice from? Drugs again? You were well out of that transaction. It was thoroughly tainted.'

Howell was back at his cottage, and Doran told him their saga of bad news there. He backed up Rodney's view, preceded by one of his Welsh Dragon snorts.

'Didn't I tell you to clear out of the shop and live off the fairs and such? It was in the wind that you'd have to, sooner or later.'

'You did. Just the advice I gave to Meg.'

'Well, then?'

'But Howell, we've got to *live*. There aren't any good fairs this side of Easter, and I can't afford to start buying things in.'

'What about that oil we found at Stargate. Did you ever get somebody else to vet it?'

Doran smiled ruefully. 'Yes, old Isaac did it for me. Absolutely no joy. Not remotely in his league. Wouldn't even offer it as a furnishing piece.'

She surveyed the Lizzie Siddal look-a-like again, newly returned from Bond Street and still leaning despondently against her tree. Doran surveyed her without affection.

'I got a good idea,' Howell said, though quite obviously avoiding her eye. 'I'll stake you. An account in your name, to draw against when you need new stock. Pay it back as you sell. No strings, no conditions, no interest.'

'Howell! I couldn't. I mean, you couldn't.'

'How d'you know? I got pay, and commissions, and bonuses. I'm loaded.'

But neither cajolery nor bullying would move Doran. She would no more borrow from a friend than Rodney would.

'We both believe in miracles, you see,' she explained.

'Like another Rossetti turning up? A proper one next time? Good luck, then, *merch* – but when it doesn't, remember I offered.'

CHAPTER NINE

St Crispin's bellringers, captained by Sam Eastry, had decided to make themselves the best in Kent. For six hours on the first Saturday of February they put all their strength and skill into a practice ring which filled the skies. The marathon was shared by another crack team, from the North of the county, who were to stay overnight for the Family Service at ten next morning.

Sam was justly proud of their performance. He thought fondly of it on his way to early Communion, still hearing the bells in his head.

The morning was silent, as Sunday mornings usually were in Abbotsbourne. If anyone was about yet they were not showing any signs, other than smoke from some chimneys. But from the far gate of the churchyard he could see two or three of the devout entering the church porch, a thin veil of ground mist between him and them, pearling the crooked old gravestones and bare trees. The grass was not so well kept as it had been in Rodney's time as vicar, and Sam noticed with extra disapproval that there were a few pieces of litter about – chocolate wrappers, a fag packet, a bottle, signs that the present incumbent was not too strict about the young using the churchyard for larking about. One of these days, or nights, it would lead to a window getting broken, and another appeal for the restoration fund.

Worse than litter – one of them was still there, lying on a table-top tomb. Passed out, and left by his mates to sleep it off, rather than bother carrying him home.

From his time on the force, and with a teenage son, Sam knew plenty about juvenile waywardness; but his Ben, even when passing through his worst phase, wouldn't have got too drunk to get home, or to a friend's. He would certainly not have slept off a booze-up on top of one of these tombs. Ben's own sister Jane was buried nearby, in the small newer section, and in earlier years his father had spent a lot of time strolling in the churchyard, trying to make out the almost illegible epitaphs on the older stones. Sam was familiar with many of the families whose names still lived on. The particular tomb he now approached bore the names of John Peacocke, Susan, Elizabeth, Matthew. They wouldn't have approved of a drunk sleeping it off on their stone.

Getting nearer, through the mist-wet grass, Sam was surprised to see the figure looked female – long hair, at any rate, and a bluish-green gown or cloak. He gave warning of his approach.

'Come on, out of it. Wakey-wakey.'

The figure remained still. Sam touched it on the shoulder – and knew at once that this sleeper would never wake again.

The face was male, stubble-chinned, though the rest of the features had been grotesquely made up to look feminine. The heavy eyebrows had been thickened with cosmetic pencil, the mouth was a huge cupid's bow of scarlet lipstick, and the cheeks were covered in what Sam thought of as pancake foundation, of a brunette tint. The shut eyes were blue-shadowed on the lids. Altogether, the effect was horrible enough to draw a grunt from the experienced Sam.

The long black hair was very tightly waved, parted in the centre and drawn in two loops low on the forehead. It looked unreal. It was. A slight pull brought it loose.

Without removing the wig, Sam could see a close-shaved head under it. A skinhead.

Never had Sam regretted so much the absence of his old walkie-talkie. It was essential that he stay on the spot, essential that he summon police help. He weighed the options open to him. The churchyard was now completely empty, except for himself. He glanced again at the awful mask, noticing the mist-moist on the fake hair, the smudge of green where one cheek had been pressed against the tombstone, one hand, large, with neglected nails. Very delicately he pushed back the fold of cloak over the wrist and inspected the arm. It was as he thought.

The congregation of six and the celebrant, the Reverend Edwin Dutton, were severely shaken to hear Sam's voice from behind them, at the south door.

'I'm very sorry to disturb you, but it's an emergency.'

Back on guard at the side of the departed Peacockes and their ghastly companion, Sam watched the line of worshippers leave the church. Frustrated worshippers, for Dutton had cancelled the service with a brief blessing, and himself gone back to the vicarage to telephone the police. Every one, leaving, turned their head towards where Sam was standing. If good manners had permitted, they would have joined him, to see for themselves and ask questions; but Abbotsbourne knew better than to do that.

Among them were the Kinchens, mother and daughter, Louise and eighteen-year-old Ellen, a first-year medical student. Louise lived on excitement. As they reached their gate she said, 'I must run in and tell Doran.'

'Why?' her daughter asked. 'What can she do?'

'That's not the point. She'll want to know, and it's her friend Sam down there. She won't mind it being early, they don't sleep in like our lot.' And, turning her back on Magnolia House, full of snoring teenage students, she rapped incisively at the knocker on the Chelmarshes' back door.

Doran answered. She was wearing a picturesque but ancient garment of the kind once known as housegowns, and her pale face was still softened with sleep. Rodney, at the kitchen table, raised his head from the middle pages of his newspaper. Kit had brought a toy car to the table and was loading it up neatly with bits of breakfast.

'Louise! Come in. Anything wrong?'

'I won't come in, really, but I thought I ought to give you a knock. There's something extraordinary going on down at the church. Ellen and I were there for early Eucharist, and Father Dutton had just got to the Collect – or what I think must be the Collect, because these services are all so different from one Sunday to another nowadays – and in burst your friend Sam, who used to be the local copper, and said there'd been a death in the churchyard, and would somebody go and fetch the police.'

'Death?' Kit's hands lifted from the toy truck of muesli.

The Kinchens' brood may have been brought up cheerfully enough on medical horrors, but Kit had not. Doran gently impelled their neighbour backwards out of the door, jerking her head at Rodney as she did so. He followed them, out of Kit's earshot.

'Lying on one of those flat tombs. Young, I think. We couldn't go and look properly, of course,' Louise was still talking. 'But I thought you'd want to know because it was you two who found that other poor girl in the river.'

Doran was startled. 'Was this a girl?' she asked quickly.

'Well, I don't know. We couldn't see from that

distance. Somehow one always tends to think of girls and women in these cases – the rape factor, I suppose.'

'Well, it's thoughtful of you to come and tell me, Louise.' Doran was edging her neighbour back in the direction of her own house. Louise was content to go, happy now that she had passed on a piece of news that was too exciting to keep to herself.

'Oh dear,' Rodney said to Doran.

They continued to linger outside, in spite of the cold mist.

'I must go down,' she said.

'No. It's nothing to do with us, whatever it is. Nothing at all.'

'How do you know?'

'Why should it have?'

'I – have a feeling. Because of – the other.'

She shivered suddenly, and moved back towards the warm kitchen. Her answer disturbed Rodney. Since the car crash, and Greg Kinchen's comment about her frail condition, he had been trying to ensure that nothing should upset her in any way. It had even made him less than cordial towards Ancilla Ireland when she had arrived to stay with them this weekend; though he had to admit that she had come because Doran had asked her, and her presence seemed to have an enlivening effect. Ancilla had proved no trouble, hadn't kept them up till all hours, wanting to talk, but had been happy to go off to bed when they did, after sharing their customary nightcap of whisky and hot water. He remembered Ancilla's presence now, and tried to use it.

'What about your friend? She'll be down to breakfast soon.'

'She won't mind, I'm sure. Just show her where everything is.'

'Hm. I recall Howell staying that time, and offering to

help, and not being able to find *anything*, except the bottles.'

'Yes, well,' she reminded him, 'women aren't like that – in case you hadn't noticed.'

Sketchily dressed, Doran hurried through the empty streets and the Square, where only the newsagent and stationer's shop was open. There was an ambulance at the churchyard gate, a police car, and a civilian one with a camera tripod and lights on the back seat. A constable was turning would-be sightseers away. He was reluctantly convinced by Doran's explanation that she had an urgent message for Sam, and, to mutters of resentment from some of the crowd, let her through.

Sam was on the edge of the knot of figures moving round the Peacocke tomb. He was keeping a tactful distance, as befitted one no longer on the force, but he was watching attentively. Doran caught his arm. He was not wholly astonished to see her.

'You've heard quickly.'

She was panting, pink-cheeked from hurrying. 'The next-door people told us. I had to see for myself. What's happened? Who is it?'

'Come round this way,' Sam said. 'Mustn't go closer. They're still taking photographs.'

One of the uniformed men looked up and frowned as they moved, but recognized Sam and turned back to what he was doing. Sam led Doran by the arm to a point from where she could see the figure lying on the tomb, lit every few moments by the blue-white flare of a flashbulb.

'My God!' he heard her exclaim, and felt her hand tighten hard on his wrist.

Kit had been taken to Sunday school rather earlier than he liked, but his mother had been unusually firm about it. She, Rodney and Ancilla were sitting over coffee in the living room.

'It was Jane Morris,' she said again. 'I mean it was meant to look like Jane. Jane as Proserpine, Astarte, Guinevere, anyone, painted by Rossetti, or Morris, or whoever. One couldn't mistake her – the long ripply hair and the arch of the upper lip. But this was a *man*, made up as a horrible caricature. A man. They couldn't find a woman to kill this time among the junkies, so they did the best they could.'

She started to laugh. Rodney, who had unobtrusively put a tot of brandy into her coffee, wondered whether he had been wise.

'Yes,' Ancilla said soothingly. 'Very nasty. But it wasn't anyone you knew, was it, so there's no need to upset yourself about it, Doran. In fact, calm down,' she added more firmly.

Rodney, distressed enough himself, approved her common-sense approach. He thought it was something of a providence, having this level-headed guest in the house just now.

He pronounced their private calmative. ' "Margaret – pray recollect yourself – Basingstoke, I beg! If you don't Basingstoke at once, I shall be seriously angry." '

Doran's laughter stopped. She shook herself, cat-like. ' "Basingstoke it is," ' she answered.

Ancilla's face showed total incomprehension. So, thought Rodney, with a tinge of satisfaction, she doesn't share all Doran's tastes, as I've been led to believe.

'Sorry,' he said. 'In-joke. Gilbert and Sullivan, *Ruddigore*, Mad Margaret.'

'Oh!' Ancilla admitted, 'I've missed out on them.'

'Oddly enough, it works,' Doran said. 'It's a sort of mantra to stop Margaret going off in hysterics when she gets excited. I didn't mean to make a spectacle of myself

– I apologize. It was just a bit overwhelming – so extremely grotesque. Anyway, you've got to agree with me, both of you – this is all too much to be a coincidence. The portrait I found, the Hollyer, the corpse dressed as Ophelia – now this one. Someone's been arranging things.'

'Not at all,' Rodney said, shaking his head. 'As we've said before, how could anyone possibly, remotely, have arranged for us to find that girl's body? We'd only just decided to go for a walk. In fact, I remember now, we decided the day before, when you got a bit low, mousing around Rossetti's grave.'

'I'm sure it wasn't meant for you,' Ancilla agreed. 'Perhaps someone wanted to attract attention for some reason.'

Against his intention, Rodney let himself join in the speculation.

'Why in that way?' he asked. 'Why make her up as Ophelia? And why get this one up to look like Jane Morris? Why not dump him on Rossetti's grave, instead of in our out-of-the-way churchyard?'

'Too public,' Doran answered readily. 'Too much visited, that other one. Anyway, maybe they'd have had trouble getting it there. Ours is nice and secluded. But why the costume and the make-up? What is someone trying to say? Something about Lizzie Siddal and Jane Morris?'

'Hardly,' Rodney said. 'How many people have heard of either of them?'

'*I* have,' Doran reminded him tensely. 'Why is all this happening on *my* patch, if there's no connection? One thing's for sure, I'll have to go to the police this time, in case they don't spot the Janey Morris connection.'

Rodney could only agree. If it helped her to tell the

police what she knew, and perhaps they didn't, it would help get it off her chest.

'Why not do it now?' Ancilla suggested. 'By telephone.'

Rodney returned her a nod of thanks, as Doran got up and went out to the hall phone.

The ear of the Eastgate police station wasn't, after all, attuned to information about Pre-Raphaelite likenesses. The officer who answered her call took down what she said, then read his note back to her: Morris, Jane, artist's model, Victorian, deceased been made up to resemble her. That was all? He would pass it on – for what it was worth, his tone said.

'Fair enough,' she admitted to the others. 'What should he be expected to make of it? Some nutter rambling on. There's nothing else for it – I'll have to go down there and explain in detail, with diagrams.'

Rodney's heart sank again. 'Diagrams?'

'Pictures. Colour illustrations of Janey, in the books. That should convince them I'm not raving, when they compare. In fact, I'll show them the Millais Ophelia as well – apologize for not pointing that out before.'

Rodney managed not to remind her that it was Sunday. It was their fixed treat day: the savoury aroma from the kitchen permeating the house, the traditional pre-lunch gin and tonic – most relaxing drink of the week – then the papers, and a settling walk, sometimes with Kit, sometimes just alone. He used to look forward to it after morning service, and did so even more now that he was unemployed on all but one Sunday a month, and missed his former routine.

Ancilla must have read his mind. 'Of course you must go, Doran,' she said. 'I'll see to the lunch, if Rodney will let me. Or are you the chef, Rodney? I'm sure you're brilliant.'

'Me? Good heavens, no. I can do an emergency snack, but a roast . . . !'

It seemed as good a compromise as he would get. Women, he thought. They could be so catty, and Doran had never been over-enthusiastic about her own sex, or had close women friends. Yet she suddenly takes up with this kindred spirit, whom he had come to appreciate as all he had been told she was. And now she's handing her kitchen over to her.

> 'What perfect joys that man attend
> Who has a faithful female friend . . .'

A pleasing premonition came to him that Ancilla would mix a perfect gin and tonic, too.

Inspector Harvey Claybourne liked working down at the nick on Sunday mornings. Things tended to be quietish, especially in winter. It was a good time to get through the accumulated paperwork that clogged up the week, before an evening out with his new wife.

The lad on the desk could deal with most of the public business that came on a Sunday morning: complaints of wild Saturday-night incidents, boastful confessions to well-publicized crimes, people wanting to air strange theories. Only the ones that seemed to need taking seriously got passed on to him after being referred first to the duty-sergeant.

Claybourne looked warily at the attractive woman (too thin for his taste, though) who had been let in, clutching an armful of what turned out to be books about art. Something about the body at Abbotsbourne, the sergeant had said, with his head round the door. He thought the inspector ought to see her.

'Do you know about this body found at Abbotsbourne?' Doran was asking now.

156

'That there's been one found, yes.' Claybourne looked again at her name on the trade card she had given him.

'Will they bring it in here?'

'No. To the mortuary.'

'Will you go to see it there?'

'Very unlikely. I'm on station duty.'

'But someone from the police will go, of course?'

He answered patiently, 'Most likely CID – detectives.'

'Oh. Well, I wonder if you, or they, would care to look at these pictures? They may help to identify the body.'

Sceptical though he was about any link between the classy volumes she was opening, and what he'd heard of the deceased, he humoured her. The plates she had marked with slips were all of the same woman, a heavy, solemn-looking type, long thick neck, a throat verging on nodular goitre, which Claybourne knew of from medical books, but had never seen, because it was rare nowadays. He recognized the crimped hair from having had a girlfriend who wore it like that and who had left it in plaits all night to achieve the effect, which he remembered as being grotesque and Topsy-like.

This woman whose pictures he was being shown had a very strange upper lip, shaped like a bow and far too big. On the whole, he would put her down as a gipsy type – if it mattered.

He nodded. 'All right. I'd know her again.'

'Now this.' Doran showed him a plate in another volume.

A redhead, floating on her back, with a lot of flowers and reeds round her, and her mouth open. Drowning? Maybe singing. He had seen this picture before. Of course – in the file of Victim One.

'Ophelia, by John Millais,' Doran helped him. 'The model's name was Lizzie Siddal. The other one is Jane

Morris, wife of William Morris, the designer and poet who . . .'

She saw the film of boredom coming over the policeman's eyes. Quickly she told him the details that she and Rodney had kept to themselves about the way the corpse in the river had been dressed.

It seemed to her a long recital. 'I suppose we should have mentioned it, but we weren't questioned, and it all seemed too fanciful to volunteer,' she apologized finally.

But Inspector Claybourne wasn't looking critical, and was clearly no longer bored. He was all alertness and intelligence – because she had just given him exclusive information about two linked murders.

What had begun as an interview that had been dutiful on Doran's part and sceptically polite on Claybourne's was transformed into an inquisition. He called in a woman police officer, who took a seat at the keyboard of a desk-top computer. A young constable brought in a cup of tea for Doran, and a coffee for her questioner. Sunday morning at the nick had suddenly perked up.

Taken down by the WPC on her green screen, Doran's full account of what she now thought of as the Pre-Raphaelite Connection included her dealings with Ralph Janner and her visits to the Mill House. Claybourne seemed keenly interested in this aspect. Was she sure she had never met Janner anywhere before? Heard of him, as dealer, collector, writer of articles in specialist magazines?

'You must get to a lot of auctions, viewings, and so forth,' he suggested. 'Could he have been at one of them?'

She shook her head. 'I'm sure I'd never seen him – though . . .'

'Yes?'

'Well, at first glance his face did look vaguely familiar.

Then I realized it was because he's a bit like Burne-Jones.'

'Burne-Jones?'

'Another of the Pre-Raphaelites.'

Claybourne raised his eyebrows, as though to suggest that the proliferation of Pre-Raphaelite associations was going a bit far. But he asked, 'Could there be any relationship between Burne-Jones and Janner?'

'I hadn't thought of that. I did mention the resemblance to him, but he made nothing of it. My imagination, I suppose. His house was very atmospheric.'

'In what way?'

It led to her detailing her second visit there, including her noticing the hay-like smell, and suspecting that someone had been smoking cannabis. The questions came thick and fast then, and the WPC's fingers moved fast on the quietly clattering keys. How did Doran know what smell cannabis left? Had she first-hand experience of its use? Had she noticed any other sign of it there, or anything else that might indicate drugs? What, by the way, was her own tolerance of medical drugs?

His manner was less casually polite, now that he was being brisk and forthright, than when he had been half bored. Doran was beginning to feel exasperated by the line of questioning which concerned herself. She saw him consult one of the documents the WPC had brought in with her and put on his desk.

'You were breath-tested after your car crash, but the result showed no alcoholic intake.'

'As I said, the wine was the non-alcoholic sort. I certainly wasn't drunk.'

'So you conclude that he must have drugged it?'

'I'm sure.'

'Why?'

He tipped his head back and regarded her under his

eyelids, in a way he had seen done very effectively in TV police dramas.

'He – wasn't best pleased that I got up and left so suddenly.'

'In other words, you think Janner had it in mind to drug you further, if you'd stayed?'

'Not only *drugged*,' Doran answered.

He sat up again. 'Ah. Would you say Janner was a dangerous man?'

After a moment's thought she said, 'Yes, I would. At least, he could be, given the chance.'

Claybourne excused himself and went out. The WPC still concentrated on her machine, running back pages and correcting mistypes. Doran wondered whether she hadn't gone rather far in condemning Ralph Janner like that, on the basis of mere suspicion? She almost asked the uniformed girl if she would erase those last questions and answers, but she knew she wouldn't. Anyway, they were lodged also in the memory of that other computer, Inspector Claybourne's mind.

She had committed herself thoroughly now. She tried to imagine what trouble it might lead to. If details of her encounters at the Mill House ever became public they would set all Abbotsbourne talking – and whispering. She pictured neighbours' looks, and the Duttons' studied smiles of forgiveness. She wondered what it might do to Rodney and Kit.

Claybourne soon returned, carrying another folder. He opened it on his desk and looked at her over it. He smiled.

'You may like to know that we're already aware of the Ophelia association with that first body.' He held up a photocopy of the Millais painting. 'We may not be connoisseurs of art, but we aren't altogether philistines, either. One bright boy got on to the intended mock-up, which wasn't as obvious as you might think, when the body wasn't floating on its back.'

Of course, she realized. To eyes not filled with art, Victim One must have appeared no more than a snub-nosed, freckled girl, dressed in tatty lace.

'Then it might help – to find whoever was responsible for that death, and perhaps this latest one?'

'It might indeed.'

It was only on the way home later that she remembered telling Sam Eastry about the significance of the dead girl's costume. Perhaps he'd passed the word on to one of his old pals. Ah, well, let them take the credit for their perception. It didn't matter, so long as it helped get results.

'How was lunch?' she asked Rodney when she got home, much too late to join them in it.

Before dismissing her, Claybourne had taken her down to the station canteen, where she was faced with a substantial, though not very tempting, mixed grill. He couldn't stay to join her, and she was rather glad. She had had enough of questions. The interrogation, though not hostile, had left her feeling drained, as though she had just undergone some intensive medical examination. She ate what she could, then quickly found her way out of the police station, before he could appear again with 'just one or two further little points'.

Rodney made a wry face in reply. 'Well – substantial.'

She was almost relieved to hear that Ancilla hadn't turned out to be a brilliant chef, like the polymath Tiggy, who had stayed with them on what had nearly been a disastrous passage in their marriage. Or like Howell's fantastic mother, who had quite a different way with food, that made Doran feel like a Cordon Beige.

It was more relief just to be at home, except that she

would have to tell Rodney that the press might strike at any moment, now she had talked. He was in a receptive mood, concerned for her long ordeal, noticing her haggard look. They were in the kitchen. Ancilla was in the drawing room, watching TV with Kit.

'I do understand why you had to do it,' he said when she had finished her story. 'I wasn't worried about publicity, only what all this would do to you. As it has. Now that it's all out, I do entreat you to leave it to the police, darling. It seems to me that Janner *must* be behind it. If so, they'll get him. We can't – we haven't the machinery. So *will* you drop it?'

'Yes. Only – that girl. She was so young, and someone had manipulated her into drugs, and then into death, and made a mockery of her. I *would* have liked to do something about that.'

'Remember that little thing of St Paul's? "Vengeance is mine: I will repay, saith the Lord." '

'Yes, but He doesn't always, does He? Or not so that anyone would notice. Well, I don't want to think about it at the moment. I must go and be sociable to Ancilla. Sorry about your lunch, but you wouldn't have liked mine, either.'

'Oh, don't apologize,' Ancilla assured her. 'It was no trouble. We enjoyed ourselves, didn't we, Kit?'

Perhaps he was too absorbed in the screen to respond.

'I haven't spent a family Sunday like this for – oh, years,' Ancilla added.

Kit suddenly came alive. 'She hasn't anyone much to play with,' he reported to his mother, 'and she can't keep cats at home, but some day she's going to have a lady like Vi to live in, when she can afford to, and then she can have two cats, or three, those fat grey ones with yellow eyes . . .'

He turned back to the television. Ancilla laughed. 'It's perfectly true,' she told Doran. 'When I make my fortune on the pools or Ernie I'm going to move further out and find some home-body to share with. But not yet.' She glanced at her watch. 'And meanwhile, I have to get going. I've a huge catalogue proof to finish reading, and if I don't do it by tonight it will spill over into tomorrow. Anyway, you'll want to be by yourselves, after you've had to be away so much today.'

This was so exactly what they both felt that they made only the merest conventional resistance. Yet, after they had seen her off at the gate, Doran said, 'In a funny way I'm sorry she had to go. The perfect stay – one night, one lunchtime, home after tea. For once, I could have taken more.'

'Not like you at all,' Rodney said as they went in. 'A nice enough woman, if deficient as a cook – but what is it she does for you, particularly? Do you really find she's on your wavelength?'

'Not yours, I gather, but mine, yes. And she really seems to care about me . . .'

'*I* care,' Rodney said, fiercely for him. 'Kit cares. Who else do you want?'

Doran didn't answer at once. Then she said, 'I don't know. All nonsense, of course. But somehow she raised my value, in my own eyes. I think that's what it is. She says all the right things that make me feel good. She said everything about the house at first sight that I'd want anyone to say, but they never do. The furniture, the pieces, my fans. And she was so nice to Kit – and Tybalt, who doesn't go out of his way to make strangers welcome.'

'Well, I see your point,' Rodney sighed. 'I certainly felt my ego being stroked today, though I'm used to that from cleric-loving ladies, of course.'

'I think she was sent to me.' Doran's voice had gone dreamy. 'Just at the right time. It's quite true what Greg Kinchen said – I am at a low ebb. I can do with all the support I can get. Or does that sound like a hypochondriac talking?'

'Yes, it does. I hope she told you to get your hair done, and have that ginger dye washed out. Frankly, it makes you look awful. Go and get it permed.'

'Well, *thanks*!' she responded resentfully. 'I don't need a perm. My hair curls naturally.'

He had successfully roused her, and carried on.

'A cross between Lillian Gish in *Broken Blossoms*, and Bunthorne being Early English. Come out of it, do, there's a good girl. And by the way, unless I don't hear the name Rossetti for at least a week I shan't be responsible for the consequences.'

The telephone rang. Rodney beat her to it.

'Mr Chelmarsh?' he heard. 'The Reverend Rodney Chelmarsh? I wonder if we could just have a word. This is the *Daily Standard*, Crime Desk. About a body you and your wife came across last month – something to do with the artist Rossetti . . .'

CHAPTER TEN

That was only the beginning. Now that local stringers had alerted the national press they were all getting their competitive teeth into what was variously described as a double murder mystery of a character gruesome, bizarre, strange, Victorian, twisted, ghastly, and other adjectives peculiar to individual newspapers. The tabloids revelled in the fancy-dress element, the drugs and the suggestion of perversion, which they deduced from the female costume on a male corpse. The eclectics went for artistic aspects, which showed their awareness. The paintings were much reproduced, the Millais *Ophelia* and those of Jane which best showed up the hair, the bow mouth, and the eyebrows. One Sunday arts supplement chose to show its readers a half-page *Astarte Syriaca* as excuse for a discussion of the painter's sexuality.

'She is a goddess, gazing, or rather glaring, at her worshippers. The canvas is six feet high, so that, worshipper or not, one must look up at her. The head is too small for the body, even with its fall of frizzled hair, surrounding a neck anything but "flower-stem-like". The "love-freighted lips", as Rossetti called them in an accompanying sonnet, look as though Astarte has just enjoyed an aperitif of human blood. The bare shoulders are strapping enough for an old-style docker, and the other charms she is about to unveil – her robe will fall off any minute now – are hinted to be correspondingly robust.

' "Her two-fold girdle clasps the absolute boon of

bliss," the poet drools on, fuelled (this is a late work, 1875–77) by excess of chloral. The year after completing it Rossetti became ill enough to be ordered by his doctors to quit London for the country.'

'Well!' Doran slammed down the newspaper. 'Talk about filthy minds! Not but what there isn't a grain of truth in it. She does look like a female impersonator on a bump-and-grind routine strip.'

'Bloody ugly, you ask me,' said Howell, who had brought this particular paper round. 'Right, whoever painted that had to be up to the eyebrows in the stuff. Silly bugger,' he added virtuously.

Doran shut the supplement on Astarte's malignantly compelling gaze. 'One does wonder what poor Janey thought about it. Not a lot, I expect. She was a very ordinary, usual woman, just your average livery-stable keeper's daughter, not cut out for notions of being a goddess or queen or mega-scale love object. She must have suffered agonies of boredom from both Dante Gabriel *and* William Morris. She'd have been better off with another livery-stableman, or a groom.'

'Jockey, could be,' Howell suggested. 'Jockeys only think about horses and prize-money. A jockey wouldn't go round trying to turn birds into goddesses.'

The telephone rang. Another journalist wanted to interview Doran, this time in the Tate Gallery, where she could give her own views on the Pre-Raphaelite collection, no doubt heavily guided by the interviewer towards the scandalous ingredients.

'All right. Why not?' she agreed. Then, to Howell, 'Free publicity, all of it. Why not cash in? It means being away from the shop again, but do you know, I've sold every picture I had in stock already, and you remember how awful some of them were. People seemed convinced they must be Pre-Raphs, because of what they've half read about me and them. Yes, I *will* go, and point out anything discreditable I can find, plus some bits I bet nobody's ever thought of. Serve old Gabriel right.'

'Don't you go getting yourself a bad name,' Howell told her primly. 'And don't wear that smoky grey colour you've been going around in. It doesn't do a lot for you, and he's sure to have a photographer.'

He had recently insinuated himself among the members of the firm who supervised the photography for catalogues, thereby assuming, in his own eyes, the mantles of Snowdon and Lichfield.

But Doran always heeded his opinions – well, sometimes. For the Tate interview she wore her best dress, a cloud-soft mohair by Jean Muir, cut on simple, pure lines, and of a delicate pale turquoise. It had cost 75p in a church fair, and she had never succeeded in working out who in Abbotsbourne's limited and far from wealthy population could possibly have owned from new anything so expensively perfect.

It added to the confidence she was already acquiring about talking to the press. Her interviewer proved not to be the brash youth or jeaned feminist she had half expected, but a tall, heavily built man in his thirties, with an impressive black moustache and wearing a dark blue pinstripe suit. His name was Todd Graeme. Far from imposing salacious hints on her he asked only the sort of questions that encouraged her to talk seriously about the pictures. On *Beata Beatrix* she found herself chatting fluently about the red dove, symbolical of death; and on the problem picture *Too Late* she surprised herself with arguments she had never considered before about the possible solution to the puzzle of the consumptive woman and the slightly repulsive child.

'I meant to be much ruder about Rossetti,' she told

Todd, after he had put away his little recorder and thanked her.

'Why?'

'Because he was a total wimp. He didn't have the moral courage to save himself from drink and drugs, and he certainly didn't save poor Lizzie from anything.'

'You have quite a thing about Lizzie, haven't you?'

'A thing? Perhaps I have. She seems to have been so very badly done to.'

'Perhaps we can chat about that some more over lunch, then?'

The restaurant he took her to was the gallery's own, in the basement, spacious and decorative, and not too crowded. She scarcely noticed the food, but enjoyed Todd's company and the laconic manner which she could see covered both worldliness and erudition. He listened with silent attention to her account of her disappointment over the Hollyertype.

'I did a piece about them once,' he surprised her. 'Believe me, you were far from the first to get taken in.'

'I know. It hurts, though. Unprofessional. The worst part was what happened afterwards.' She described how she had returned the picture, and got drugged and nearly killed for her pains. 'I hope they get him. Only, the last I heard, he'd done a flit. The police have been on to the house's owner. Nobody knows where he's gone.'

She had not seen her companion react to her passing mention of Ralph Janner by name, coupled with the Burne-Jones resemblance she'd noticed. She was astonished when he said, 'I might know where he is.'

'*You?* You know him?'

'A lot of people do. Not always as Ralph Janner, though. And you're right – he's a seriously elusive character.'

She waited for more, but he didn't go on. She had to ask, 'Is – is he into drugs, do you know?'

'I don't know anything, until I've seen it for myself and can prove it. Rely on hunches – circumstantial evidence – and you and your paper can be landed with a libel suit and hefty damages. Let's just say I shouldn't be surprised.

'By the way,' he added, 'that resemblance to Burne-Jones . . .'

'I didn't mean *very* like. Only in passing.'

'But you're right. It's one of his "looks", and he plays up to it. Odds are now, if he suspects anyone's after him, he'll have switched to his William Morris look. He does, from time to time.'

'I don't believe it!' Doran exclaimed. But, on reflection, she could. Janner's straggling beard could soon become one that fringed the entire jaw. A frizzy perm would transform his hair to 'Topsy' Morris's curls. Overdressing and perhaps padding would produce a fuller figure. Why he should go to those particular lengths she couldn't imagine, but it would certainly serve the purpose of a 'seriously elusive' character.

'And you think you know where he is?' she prompted.

'Where he *might* be. One of his places. Don't ask me to tell you, though. You might get tempted, though you've had enough experience already to know better than to go calling on him.'

'But the police ought to know,' she protested. 'From what you've said, he sounds some sort of menace.'

Todd said meaningfully, 'I haven't *said*. Maybe hinted, but I'd deny that in court. However . . .'

'Yes?'

'I don't owe him any favours. He's a hard man to pin down, and if they're looking for him in connection with something specific that might be possible to prove for once, then a little anonymous help might be indicated. *Strictly* anonymous, though. You'll have to promise me you won't say a word about where it came from.'

'Of course I won't. Are you going to speak to the police?'

'Just leave it there, shall we? I'll see to it. It'll be rather a pleasure.'

Doran soon learned that he had kept his word. Sam Eastry had news for her as they leaned on his paddock fence on Sunday morning, watching Jennifer riding Brandy round and round. He had telephoned her to meet him there, and she'd known from his tone that he had something of significance to tell her.

'The Met have tracked down that chap of yours – Janner. Rented flat in Kentish Town, owned by a big group who don't want to know who their tenants are, so long as they pay up.'

She was careful not to ask how he had been traced, or whether he had been in disguise when found.

'Old office building converted into flats,' Sam was rambling on, enjoying renewed contact with police work. 'Nothing grand, but not too far downmarket. Tenants don't seem to notice one another, but seems he had a lot of late-night visitors, clattering up and down the stairs.

'Visitors?'

'Kids, mostly. Seems you were right about drugs, Doran. They found plenty there. He must have spotted the Met boys watching the place, and decided it was too risky to go back in. They gave him twenty-four hours then moved in. He hadn't been back, and the drugs were there. He must have meant to come back for them, but saw it had become too hot.'

'But he's given them the slip again?' She was very tempted to mention the William Morris transformation, in case they were working on a wrong description, but Sam referred to it before she could, as part of the anonymous information that had reached the police from 'a contact of a contact'.

'What an extraordinary thing,' she said. 'To go to all that trouble – disguise and so forth. Sam . . . you don't suppose he could have been mixed up in either of those murders?'

Or both, she wondered, and realized sickeningly how vulnerable she'd been, alone with him at the Mill House. Had she been in danger of being made a third victim?

'I don't know anything about that,' Sam replied, 'So far as I've heard, they could have been a bit of "fun" gone wrong. After all I've seen over the years, nothing would surprise me at what some people get up to.'

'And that,' she said to Rodney afterwards, 'is really full stop for me. I gather they're not telling the press about looking for him. Playing it down, I suppose. As for those two victims . . .'

'None of your business,' he told her firmly. 'I'm glad you've seen the light at last. Let it be full stop indeed.'

He hurried off to a parish council meeting at Elvesham, leaving her to sit on thoughtfully at the uncleared lunch table. She appreciated Rodney's concern, as always – but he had misunderstood her. By 'full stop' she hadn't meant she was finished with the whole business. She'd meant she had reached a dead end, beyond which she couldn't see any way to go. The police were on the trail of the slippery Janner, and investigating the two deaths. Still feeling herself somehow involved, and certain that there was more than coincidence between many of the details, she was restless for some progress, and wondering what she might be able to do to make things move.

Each way she considered seemed blocked. She couldn't expect Sam to keep pumping his mates on her behalf.

She knew that Todd Graeme would not welcome any more questions from her, and almost certainly wouldn't answer them.

Then she thought of Greg Kinchen. There was one detail she'd been contemplating asking him, as a medical man, but recent activity had kept her from finding time. It wasn't a matter for the telephone. She decided to go round next door.

Greg and Louise were both out on separate expeditions, but one of their medical student lodgers, Vic, was expecting Dr Kinchen back very soon. He was just making some tea and invited Doran to join him in a cup. She was glad to accept. Vic was a short, chubby, almost dimpled youth, with a misleading choirboy aspect.

He led her into the room used undiscriminatingly by the Kinchen family and their lodgers. The table, where he began laying out tea things, chattering meanwhile, was already occupied by a skull, a dish of ancient-looking bones, and something floating in a jar, from which Doran averted her eyes. Vic noticed her glance and moved it away. The bones remained, though.

'Nice, aren't they?' he said cheerfully. 'They mostly hand out plastic specimens, but these are the real thing. A friend of my Dad's gave me his skull. I mean, not *his*, but one he happened to have. Kind of him, wasn't it? Makes you feel more in touch, handling the real thing.'

'Like a full dress rehearsal, I suppose.'

Vic's lack of response revealed an untheatrical mind. He demonstrated to her rapidly the locations of the squamous suture, the external meatus, os planum, mandible, thyrohyal . . .

'Just a minute,' she interrupted, suddenly interested. 'Isn't that the same as the hyoid bone?'

He looked at her with new respect. 'That's it. It's very interesting that . . .'

'And would it take a blow to fracture it – on the side of the neck?'

'Needn't be a blow. It's often a sign of strangulation. Useful clue to the cause of death if the tissues have disintegrated. Why?' Vic beamed. He loved to be asked questions, especially informed ones.

'Nothing,' Doran said faintly. She had always imagined the Ophelia girl being struck a sharp death-blow. Now she saw a pair of hands round the frail throat, above the lace and mock jewels.

'Well, well.' Dr Kinchen stood in the doorway, unwrapping his scarf. 'What's this – an anatomy lesson?'

Vic told him, 'I was explaining my lovely skull to Doran. We were just discussing the hyoid.'

'It doesn't seem to have done her a lot of good, then.' Greg had a sharp eye for reactions. Doran threw him a grateful wince of a smile.

'Oh,' Vic said apologetically. 'I thought you were enjoying it. She was just asking me, Doctor, about . . .'

'Very much out of politeness, I'm sure. You don't find many lay people keen to hear the sort of grisly details we think nothing of. I'd advise you to remember that.' He turned to the pale Doran. 'Did you want Louise, Doran, or me?'

'You, please. If you've got a minute.'

In the upstairs room where he kept his medical books and all that went with his profession, he sat her down in a comfortable old leather chair, which had reassured many nervous patients in the days when he had done home consultations. Unwilling to retire completely, he nowadays helped himself and others by acting in a medical capacity for various charities, doing examinations for insurance companies, and standing in as locum tenens for the Health Centre. He was so much liked ('Always has time for you, has Dr Kinchen, and knows

173

when there's more to your trouble than you can tell him') that he scarcely spent a moment regretting giving up full-time work.

He seated himself beside his small desk, instead of behind it, and leaned forward with keen attention to what Doran had come, without appointment, to ask or tell.

'It's not actually about me . . .' she began to apologize.

'Isn't it? Perhaps it ought to be.'

She was much too thin, her cheekbones sharp beneath shadowed eyes, her hair – and what had she been doing to it? dull and straggling. She saw his critical look at it.

'I know it looks awful. I tried giving myself a bit of colour with those non-animal products you can get in Barminster, but Rodney and Howell both remarked on it, so I washed it out, and it seems to have gone no colour at all.'

'Not just your hair, Doran. Remember, I noticed you looking a bit off, at the Christmas Fair. It shouldn't be going on still. Are you eating properly?'

'Not fantastically.'

'Sleeping?'

'A lot of waking up and not being able to go off again.'

The doctor frowned. 'You're not my patient, but I'm going to suggest something you might take.' He scribbled, then handed the note to her. 'It's not on prescription, so you can buy it across the counter; but I think you ought to go along to the Medical Centre and let them have a look at you.' He was scribbling another note. 'This is just something that will be a good nutrient source, as well as a tonic – not that tonics exist, medically speaking.'

'Well, thank you – Greg. It always makes me feel impertinent, calling you that.'

'Never mind. I prefer it. And I can be impertinent,

oo. Your hair *is* a mess, and you need a general buck-up. Why don't you go back to Barminster and have a whole day's beauty treatment? You needn't laugh. I haven't tried it myself, but our Claudia has, right above that shop where you got your potions. She told us it made her feel wonderful, and it certainly cured her of all sorts of little ailments I knew she hadn't got, but couldn't convince her.'

'All right. Thanks. I will. But . . .'

'Of course, you didn't come to see me for beauty counselling. What was it?'

Doran hesitated. 'I – I'm not sure. At least, I wasn't, until Vic started showing me that skull. Greg, do you have any access to police files? On murder victims?'

He didn't answer at once. He thought he knew what was coming. He'd heard from Louise and others of several sensational cases in which Doran had got herself involved, before they became her neighbours. By all accounts, her curiosity had been much to blame. Could there be a hidden streak of morbidity in her? Whatever it was, he didn't want her indulging it again. Like one of Agatha Christie's characters, he didn't approve of murder. He had seen the results of it several times in his long career. It was always nasty, and sometimes very nasty indeed. In his view, the only people who should be mixed up in it were official persons – certainly not young women of sensibility, who were also wives and mothers with family responsibilities.

'I don't think I can help you on that one,' he said seriously.

'Oh dear. I hoped you could. It's about those two . . .'

'I know, I know. Our local corpses. Please listen to me, Doran . . .' he began, but she interrupted.

'I feel I have to follow up any line that might identify them. Rescue them from being just numbers on files.

What will be put on their graves? Where will they b
buried?'

'Nowhere, as yet. Until they've been identified there'
no question of burial. After that it will be up to whoeve
claims them.'

Greg glanced at his watch. Doran took the hint an
stood up.

'All right, we won't discuss it. Just tell me, because
know you know – could they have both died simply from
drug-taking over a long period?'

'It depends. Well, yes, but . . .'

'But they were both killed – strangled, or by a blow
that fractured the hyoid bone?'

'Yes,' he admitted, since she obviously knew.

'Thanks,' she said. 'I did know about the girl, but no
the boy. I'm sorry to have wormed it out of you. I won'
tell anyone you told me.'

'Goodbye,' he said with finality. 'Don't forget you
tonic. And go and be soothed at Barminster.'

For once, it was advice she was glad to take. One c
Barminster's large Georgian houses, vacant and vandal
ized before being refurbished as commercial premises
had the fragrance shop below, and, upstairs, two parlour
and four cubicles. The lighting there was restful, from
sunken stars of spotlights in the ceiling and individua
angle-lamps. The decor was a wallpaper of old roses
not, Doran was glad to see, a William Morris design
and a very faint, ineffable scent of roses had been clever
instilled in the air. *Spectre de la Rose*. She daydreamed
as she lay on her front, tingling from the jacuzzi, bein
massaged with aromatic oils by a pink-overalled girl wit
more strength in her skilful hands than her slight buil
suggested.

Doran was glad to let her mind relax and wander whe

.t would. Into its space drifted ballerinas, swans, pictures from Kit's fairy books, a Cotswold landscape from her unofficial honeymoon, a vision of Jennifer Eastry's pony frisking in his paddock on a windy March day of scudding clouds. The cathedral, majestic in winter dusk, softly floodlit. Kit walking for the first time, staggering towards her with open arms, his face half-frightened, half-delighted. Rodney batting fourth for Abbotsbourne's cricket XI, younger by ten years as he was when she had first known him, handsome and brown-faced. A beautiful Bow group she had once found almost undamaged at an executors' sale. An exhibition of tapestries she had gone to recently with Ancilla: figures in landscape, kings and queens, knights and ladies, running deer and hounds, birds as big as cows but not at all inconvenienced by it, trees and flowers in bloom for ever, while the silks and canvas endured . . .

The massage was over. She was wrapped in swathes of warm pink towelling, to recline in a comfortable tilting chair while a manicurist turned her nails into shining shells.

'You've got lovely hands,' said the girl, as though she meant it.

'Thanks to you, at the moment. I'm afraid it won't last, not when they're put to dirty work.' She explained about wood-stripping, furniture glue, china repairs, the grubbiness of old books, the frequent minor wounds incurred in removing pictures from old frames . . . That brought the Hollyertype back to mind. She wanted to dismiss it quickly, but the manicurist was asking about faking antiques and pictures. Doran had to answer.

'It's not all that easy to do, and harder still to detect, sometimes. Oil paintings, for instance. Wormholes in the frame are very suspicious. The ground on the canvas would be gesso – plaster, mixed with glue made from rabbit skin. Then you have to work out how many layers of paint have been put on over it, and whether the artist it's claimed to be by would have used so many, or so few.'

'Fascinating.' But the girl wasn't really interested. Technical details did bore people. When they asked about antiques and art, their only real concern was what they were worth. The manicurist had finished. She waited as the beautician and the hairdresser set things up for a facial and a shampoo and cut ('This length really doesn't suit your face at all, Mrs Chelmarsh'), and a light hazel-brown rinse. ('I don't think chestnut's right for you at all. I can put you back to your proper colour, if that's what you'd like.')

The infinitely delicious, soothing processes of the facial were over too soon. She viewed the results incredulously. Years seemed to have slipped away, taking her back into her days of courtship. Her skin was clear as alabaster, her eyes bright, rested, very delicately outlined, her forehead smooth.

'Wonderful!' she told the proprietress, who cleverly called herself Bella. 'But how long will it last?'

'Oh, a long time, if you keep up with the creams and other things.' She had already quietly persuaded Doran into buying three extremely expensive jars of oils and lotions, thus adding considerably to the price of the day's treatments.

'That place ought to be called the Pelican – enormous bill,' Rodney remarked, contemplating the results. 'Well worth it, though. No need to feel guilt about money spent on essential restoration. You look wonderful. Too expensive to touch.'

'I'm not. Try.'

'And radiant. "Round her head a glory, like a saint's

178

She seemed a splendid angel, newly drest, save wings, for heav'n." '

'It's a long time since Keats cropped up in the conversation.'

'Too long,' Rodney was still gazing at her, as though he hadn't seen her recently. ' "For ever shalt thou gaze, and she be fair." '

Kit looked up from a striking composition he was making in coloured chalk and bits of felt.

'Who's Skeats? Has he been here?'

'A good deal,' Rodney said. 'But you won't quite remember.' His eyes held Doran's. But for Keats and St Agnes's Eve, there might have been no Kit. 'Don't you think Mummy looks pretty?' he asked.

'Mm. Sort of clean. Did you have a special bath, Mummy?'

'You could call it that,' Rodney answered for her. 'It's a crystal fountain that comes out of a rock and falls into a beautiful pool with all sorts of colours at the bottom of it, and doves perching on the side. It's called the Bath of Venus.'

'Well, Mummy looks prettier than Miss Martin.'

'Thanks, darling. That's something, coming from you. Rodney, your description sounds like something by Alma Tadema. Lots of marble. Remember that infant's description of the nymph drawing water from a lion's-head spring? – doggy be sick into lady's potty.'

'Yes. And may we please have a ten-year ban on all references to all Victorian painters?'

'You started it.'

'I know I did, and I shouldn't have. I'm just a fraction tired of them. Let's go over to Stoner Bay and have supper at that jolly place where they welcome children so nicely, then Kit can come. It's cheap and cheerful. Would you like that, Kitten?'

Kit swept his chalks and felt off the table in his rush to embrace his father.

The post lying on the doormat appeared to be a perfectly ordinary one: bills, junk mail, an insurance statement, and an envelope in the too-familiar handwriting of one of Rodney's would-be dependants, not even a parishioner, but one who tried it on with every clergyman in the county. Rodney had responded more than once to the moving appeals, until seeing Will Hay, propped up against a bar in an old film on television: 'I have had four little tots already and am just going to have another one.' He hadn't answered any since.

Doran was about to throw this new heart-cry away unopened, then reflected that, since it was addressed to Rodney, the decision was properly his. As she picked the letter up, she found another, smaller one under it. It was addressed to her in typewritten capitals. London postmark. She turned it over curiously before taking it into the kitchen, where they opened their post together.

There was no letter inside. Just a slip of plastic card with the number 27 on it, and some smaller figures and letters, and the words BRITISH RAIL. She stared at it.

'What's this? I haven't any dealings with British Rail.'

Rodney, out of sheer curiosity, had opened the begging letter, containing a plea for ten pounds to save his old acquaintance – whom he knew for certain he had never met in his life – from starvation.

'The chap may have fallen on really hard times,' he mused. 'After crying wolf for so long. Perhaps . . .'

'Oh, Rodney, won't you ever learn? When they say there's nothing between them and the workhouse it means they're literally leaning against the workhouse door. Or it did, when there were workhouses. Never mind him, he's probably rolling in money. We can't afford him. I think I know what this is.'

'What? Oh, you mentioned British Rail. Perhaps you bought some Channel Tunnel shares years ago, and now you're rich.'

'It's the key to a station locker. You deposit something, and they give you this plastic thing, so that you're the only one who can use it to open it again.'

'Really? I've never used a locker.'

'I have. They're very useful for parking something you don't want to carry all round London, until you come back to get the train home.'

'Ah. On the principle of delivering a body in a trunk to Left Luggage, and not coming back for it, so it's stored indefinitely – or until it makes itself noticed. Austin Freeman's very good on that sort of thing. Which is the story where Dr Thorndyke finds a head in a suitcase?'

Doran contemplated the plastic slip abstractedly, having opened the envelope to look for an accompanying note, but finding none. Vi came in from the hall, unwinding the Jaeger scarf Doran had given her for Christmas and which she wore on every possible occasion. Doran held up the mystery object.

'This just came for me, Vi. Any theories?'

'Present from BR? Bit out of character for them, isn't it? You dropped it on the station, did you, and some kind soul's posted it on?'

'I didn't drop it, because I never had it. I haven't used one of those lockers for ages. Anyway, my address isn't on it. How could anyone know?'

Vi scrutinized the card. 'I can tell you one thing – it belongs to Barminster station. We often use them on market days, what with the market being on one side of the line, and the shops on the other, worth the money, though I must say I used to like the proper Left Luggage, where there was a man in charge, keeping things safe and used to tell you a bit of Barminster news, like that time there was the funny business about the man in the cathedral who . . .'

Before they could be regaled with Trollopian reminiscence, Doran interrupted, 'The puzzle is that I haven't been using the lockers. So why does it get sent to me?'

'Well, I don't know. You be careful, if you go opening it. Never know nowadays, might be a bomb, like those parcel bombs people get sent, and blown to pieces in their own home . . .'

Rodney interrupted sharply, with some distraction that sent Vi placidly away to the kitchen.

Doran was staring at the plastic key with new awareness.

'You don't think . . . ?' she said, almost to herself. 'It couldn't be Janner trying something again?'

'I don't know,' Rodney said grimly. 'But what I do know is, you're not opening that locker yourself.'

CHAPTER ELEVEN

An officer and a soldier from Bomb Disposal opened it. Doran, Rodney, and a curious crowd who had materialized from the farthest-flung parts of Barminster, watched from a very safe distance.

The metal door swung open. There was an audible, palpable hush – followed by nothing. No flash, no explosion.

They saw the officer remove something from inside. It was an old-fashioned black deep box. He seemed to take an age examining it minutely, using a doctor's stethoscope. Then he prised it open.

'It's all right,' he called to the policemen supervising the crowd. 'Just papers.'

No-one ticked them off. 'Better safe than sorry,' was the police attitude, in view of Doran's known story. All the same, she and Rodney felt ashamed. The fuss their precautions had caused would mean more press attention, just when it seemed to have petered out.

They left the scene as soon as they could, all too conscious of gapes and murmurs. Rodney drove them home quickly. Only then, in the normality of the kitchen, did they examine the packet of papers that had been within the box. The box itself, which had Doran's name on a label tied to a handle, was kept by the police, to check for fingerprints if it became necessary. They had glanced inside the package, to make sure that there was nothing other than papers, then handed it over to Doran, with instructions to report anything that might interest them.

The package had been fastened with ancient, worn string. As they unwrapped it a smell of dusty dryness wafted up, the unmistakable odour of old paper.

'Dickens and lawyers' offices,' Rodney said, determined to make light of it, now that the drama was over. 'The fust and must of Lincoln's Inn. Nothing quite like it.'

'But no moth,' Doran followed his lead. 'And no mice. What a mercy.'

'Mice would have been miracle workers to have gnawed through that box. You do the unveiling.'

On top of the bundle she disclosed lay a yellowed sheet of plain artist's paper, and under it a sheet of tissue. She lifted them off.

'Oh!'

Rodney made no sound. He was staring at a drawing that was unmistakably of Lizzie Siddal: the pure face calm, almost expressionless, the hair neat and smooth.

Speechless, Doran set it aside. Next to appear was another drawing, of Lizzie standing, her plain dress clinging to her slender figure, the hem hiding her feet, the simple round neck encircling the base of her long, lovely throat. Her hands hung by her sides, an attitude that in another could have been awkward; her pose was perfect grace.

Then there was another, of her head alone, turned away slightly from the artist; the full-lidded eyes gazing into space, or daydreaming. And yet another, a half-length, seated on a Windsor chair. And another, and another. Each bore the monogram *DGR*, and the date, 1854.

'I don't believe I'm seeing this,' Rodney said huskily.

Doran shook her head wordlessly. She was close to tears.

'They can't be more Hollyertypes – can they?' he asked, his mind racing as he wondered whether this was another cruel trick aimed at her.

'I don't think so,' she managed to reply. 'I know what to look for now, and it's not there. These are original drawings. Everything about them says they're genuine Rossettis. The age looks right, the paper – though it'll need testing. And I remember from one of the books that someone called at Chatham Place and found Dante Gabriel drawing Lizzie over and over again. He kept calling her "Guggums, wonderful lovely Guggums", while she posed patiently, though he drew like lightning. I think these may be some of those – 1854 would be about right. Oh, but look – this isn't Lizzie.'

She had reached a drawing that was on a smaller sheet of paper. It was of a different woman, with a squarish face, a voluptuous mouth, and hair frizzed out and threaded with jewels. A fur wrap was suggested in pencil strokes behind the head and neck.

'Fanny Cornforth,' Rodney said with certainty. 'The mistress. Monna Vanna, Bocca Baciata. She grew enormously fat, so he called her Elephant instead. But she stayed faithful to him to the end, and then married a publican – I think. That must be a later drawing.'

It was. The monogram had changed slightly, and the date was 1867.

'Lizzie was dead by then,' Doran reflected. 'Dead and buried – re-buried. Oh, here's Jane.'

The face was now the stern tragic one of Jane Morris, the drawing subtly coarser, the delicate touch of the Siddal portraits gone. Jane's face appeared on three separate sheets, the third being the last of the collection. Collection was what it appeared to be, each frail creamy sheet carefully protected with its own piece of tissue.

Doran replaced them carefully, in the order they had been.

'Well,' she said. 'Utterly wonderful. Unbelievable. But what's it about? Why me?' She looked to Rodney for reassurance. 'Suppose it's some kind of trap. Am I being set up for a charge of theft, or harbouring stolen goods? Are they going to come knocking on the door any minute now?'

'I don't like it,' Rodney admitted.

Nor did he, in more ways than one. It posed a threat to Doran, whether or not her half-serious guess held any possibility. Worse, it brought her back into the morbid aura of Pre-Raphaelite gloom and doom; the phosphorescent light which had gleamed on her and changed her. He feared very much for what it might do to her. The sense of evil that came to him sometimes was strong upon him.

'We must tell the police at once,' he said. 'Then they can't accuse you of having stolen property. That man of yours at Eastgate – Claybourne. Ring him now.'

Doran sighed. 'You know what they'll do – take them away. Into custody. That might be the last I see of them. I *can't* let them go just like that, after the merest glance. I've been cheated twice out of a Rossetti, and now I've got a couple of dozen. I *have* to know if they're authentic. It won't take long.'

Already her new bloom was fading. The faint lines of anxiety were back on her brow. Their private world was being invaded again by the fretful ghosts of a long-dead artist and his models. Reluctantly, because he heard the intensity in her plea, Rodney said: 'Promise, though, that the minute you know, one way or the other, you'll tell Claybourne. Solemn promise, mind.'

'All right. I've got his direct line number in my bag.'

'Where do you propose taking them? Howell's man?'

'No, better. Sacheverell Isaac. He'll know at once.'

She telephoned the Bond Street gallery immediately, but the number was engaged. After several attempts she heard the purring tones of Selina.

'Sacheverell Isaac and Partners.'

Doran identified herself. 'Is he in, by any chance? I would rather like a personal word.'

She was put through almost at once, slightly to her surprise, for Selina guarded well.

'My dear Doran.' Over the telephone the tinge of Vienna was strong in Sacheverell's gentle voice. 'What can I do for you?'

'A lot. A great favour.' Tripping over her words, she told him the history of the last few hours.

'Another Rossetti discovery – and on such a scale! Well, well. I find this quite remarkable.'

'I know,' Doran agreed. 'And I feel sure there's something a bit sinister behind it, but I just *have* to know if they're the real thing before I let them go. I'd regret it if I found out later that they're real, and I'd handed them in without appreciating what I'd had in my hands.'

'My dear, I quite understand. Do you wish to bring them to me?'

'Oh, thank you. I was wondering if tomorrow might do?'

'One moment, please.' Doran heard subdued murmuring as he consulted Selina. He came back, to say, 'I am not free tomorrow at all. However, this evening I could come to you to inspect the drawings. I think this would be a great deal safer than allowing you to bring them to me. Strange accidents can happen to travellers with valuable cargo. So, if it would be convenient to you . . . ?'

Thrilled at the prospect of the great dealer coming to her, Doran stammered out that it was certainly convenient. She started to mention trains, but he sounded unattracted by them. He said, 'I think it will be better if I drive down.'

'Are you sure? At least you'll have dinner with us?'

With a smile in his voice he answered that he would be happy to share whatever they had been going to have themselves.

'Heavens!' Doran turned to Rodney. 'You gathered all that? He'll be here in about two hours. Oh dear, we were down to spaghetti tonight. I can't give him that.'

'For a man in his rarefied atmosphere it might be quite a novelty. Unless he gets given it at home all the time.'

'No, I couldn't, with him driving down specially. I know – Vi.'

Vi graciously consented to stay on after fetching Kit home from school. Doran gave her a free hand to concoct one of her more recherché dishes, depending on what she could find in the village. The hurried shopping expedition was obviously successful, from the delicious aroma of stew coming from the kitchen. Even the would-be vegetarian Doran decided to waive her principles for once and share it.

It was just under two hours before a black Mercedes glided down Mays Lane and stopped at Bell House. Doran hurried to the gate. In the driving seat was a girl in some dark uniform, as elegant as the car. She got out swiftly and opened a rear door for Sacheverell, who bent over Doran's hand with what was not quite a kiss, but considerably more courteous and stately than a handshake. He paused to admire the house before following her in. The chauffeuse, he said, worked for a hire firm. She would stay with the car, and needed no feeding.

Sacheverell and Rodney found each other easy

company. Doran left them alone to enjoy a drink. She knew she could not relax over one herself. She wondered how she would get through dinner, waiting for the important aspect of the visit to begin with the coffee. To her relief, Sacheverell tactfully spared her the suspense.

'Is that aromatic dish which I can smell in danger of spoiling, if we delay eating it for a half hour or so?'

Doran could honestly say it wasn't. Vi had put it in the hot trolley, where it would keep perfectly. She had quietly put Kit to bed, and left discreetly without interrupting.

'Then,' said Sacheverell, 'I suggest we get over the important business first. Just an assessing glance, perhaps? Then we can talk over the meal.'

Instantly at ease again, Doran unwrapped the frail packing. The dusty smell of age had not gone. Once more, Lizzie, calm, impassive, was revealed.

Sacheverell viewed each drawing minutely, first without his glass, then through it. As he came to the point where the model changed to Fanny Cornforth he uttered a small sound of surprise or amusement. Doran hardly dared breathe. Rodney suppressed a desire to wander about the room.

After what seemed like hours, but had been only minutes, Sacheverell sat back and looked at Doran.

'I should say that we have something very remarkable here.'

She clutched Rodney's arm, as Sacheverell went on.

'To my eye – and I am not usually mistaken about such things – these drawings are by Rossetti. They are certainly of the right age, the style and materials are right, and so is the paper. Mid-Victorian. There is a slight coarseness of line that troubles me a little. It is something rather different from the blurring that comes of age.

Otherwise, I see nothing to contradict your belief that they are genuinely by Rossetti.'

'I noticed the blurring,' Doran said. 'The second time I went through them. And,' she felt she had to admit, 'the signature seems to change. I put it down to his being into heavy drugs, really ill.'

'There are signs of it in nearly all of them, I believe,' Sacheverell agreed. 'In a way, it gives them even greater authenticity. But I should still have to examine each one of them very closely to give you a firm opinion. Thank heaven I did not allow you to carry them up to town. If you wish, I will take them back with me. They will be totally safe then.'

Doran looked at Rodney. He said, 'There's rather more to it than that. Perhaps we could discuss it at table?'

Sacheverell was willing enough, and applied himself to dinner with evident enjoyment. Doran was hardly conscious of the food she was praising so highly. Rodney watched her continually, afraid of seeing the signs of what he thought of as morbid melancholia.

Sacheverell held his glass of supermarket red wine up to the light, admiring it as if it were a prized vintage. 'If they are genuine,' he said, 'you realize that they would be worth a fortune? Not a small one, but a large one.'

'We do realize,' Rodney said. 'Unfortunately, they aren't ours.'

The exact details of the windfall had been explained. Also the fact that they were bound to report to the police anything 'interesting' relating to the package they had been allowed to hold on to. If a prospective fortune didn't class as interesting, what would?

'But it is so curious that the owner, whoever that is, should have put them into your hands without identifying himself. If they are intended as some sort of gift from someone who does not suspect their true value, it would be your absolute responsibility to find who that is and return them, telling them the truth.'

'We know that,' Rodney agreed. 'Which is why we ought to go back to the police with your findings. But they wouldn't thank us for letting you take the pictures away, no matter who you were.'

'And if we hang on to them, and don't report what you've said,' added Doran, 'we might be – what is it? – compounding a felony.'

'As so should I,' the dealer pointed out, 'by knowing of their existence but not disclosing it. Perhaps they are stolen property. If so, the person who has sent you them has placed you in a very vulnerable and dangerous position.'

'It couldn't be Janner, could it?' Doran said. They had discussed that possibility thoroughly while waiting for Sacheverell to arrive.

'No, no,' Rodney said. 'Villain though he may be, he'd hardly be so simple-minded as to hope you'd get them authenticated, and sell them so that he could come down on you for his share. Assuming that they were his, anyway. He'd have to be mad to try that.'

'Well, what else is there?' Doran sighed. 'All I know is that these marvellous things have appeared from nowhere. And meant for *me*.'

Rodney quickly suggested that they move to the drawing room for coffee. He saw that the whole process was threatening to damage her still further. The sooner the things were off her hands, the sooner they could try forgetting the whole business – again. If she kept them for too long, she might become emotionally possessive.

Sacheverell had a more comforting observation to make over the coffee.

'I do not think they have been stolen by anyone capable of knowing their value. Their condition, and the way in which they were packaged, suggests them to be what we term sleepers.'

'Sleepers?' Rodney asked. It was Doran who replied.

'Objects left lying neglected for years, either because people didn't think they were worth anything, or they looked too old-fashioned . . .'

'Or,' Sacheverell put in, 'because someone once did know what they were, and, rather than destroy them, chose to put them away, out of sight.'

Doran stared at him. 'You mean – someone Rossetti had given them to himself.'

'Who knows?' said Sacheverell. 'He was a romantic, but not a philanthropist. In the mid-1850s he was getting up to four hundred pounds for an oil. A drawing would make a good deal less, but each of these represented money, which I cannot see him giving away. But again, who knows? One must be prepared to believe anything with regard to art and artists. Anything at all.'

He looked at his watch and put his coffee cup and saucer aside.

Doran asked finally, 'So, what do you advise me to do?'

He got up, 'You know already, my dear girl. Hand over this fascinating property to the police in the morning. Tell them what I have said, and add that if they wish to have them properly authenticated, I shall be pleased to advise them.'

He was gone, the sleek Mercedes already far beyond Abbotsbourne. Rodney mechanically loaded the dishwasher while Doran opened yet another tin of cat food for the stout and greedy Tybalt, who had been kept firmly in the kitchen while the drawings were on display. He was demonstrating his resentment by demanding a second supper.

Rodney inserted the last plate and slammed the machine shut.

'That's it, then. You promised to turn those drawings in as soon as you knew about them. Well, now you know.'

'Not *definitely*. He wasn't sure . . .'

'Your Mr Isaac strikes me as a man whose instinct for danger is fairly reliable. Living under Hitler did that for people, I imagine. And what he said is perfectly true. You don't want to find yourself in the dock, do you?'

'No.'

'Then we go to Eastgate in the morning.'

There was a note in Rodney's voice that was seldom there.

At Eastgate they had to wait an hour for Inspector Claybourne to come on duty. With the package of drawings safely locked in the car boot, in clear view of the police station, they walked to the nearby seafront and passed the time on a seat, overlooking the grey expanse of the Channel, saying little.

Claybourne on a weekday morning was brisker than Doran remembered from her Sunday visit. His sergeant was a woman, as smart and immaculate in her uniform as he. Together they could have modelled for a poster for police recruitment.

He knew all about the railway station locker incident. He viewed the drawings impassively.

'Not much point handing them to the fingerprint boys. Who do you say they're of?'

He took Doran through the details twice.

'And you've no idea at all who could have planted them for you to pick up?'

'Well, we don't know, but I think it may have been the man who tried to get me to sell the Hollyertype.'

Claybourne flicked a few keys, and the computer

screen provided him with a string of information.

'Janner. Wanted for possession of heroin and other substances.'

'I didn't know about that,' Doran said, not quite truthfully.

'Some were found on the premises he'd skipped from in London. We don't tell every development, you know.'

'All right. Will you tell me if he's been found yet?'

'Seems not. An elusive customer, but they're looking hard.' He gave Doran one of his sudden, uncomfortably sardonic smiles. 'I can tell you also that the staff at Barminster station have no recollection of who that locker key was issued to.'

'He may have been in disguise. I was told he had a thing about using the looks of different artists – Burne-Jones, William Morris . . .'

'You were told that, Mrs Chelmarsh?' Claybourne pounced. 'Who told you? You didn't get it from us.'

Doran looked at Rodney. He stayed silent, not prepared for once to give her any help.

She floundered, 'I – promised not to tell. It was a newspaperman. It might get him into trouble.'

Claybourne said, in an easier tone, 'You can rely on us not to involve him unnecessarily, but we've got to know. This is a criminal matter, you realize?'

Feeling traitorous, Doran named Todd Graeme and his newspaper.

Claybourne scribbled. 'That could help,' he said. 'Now, is there absolutely nobody else you connect in your mind with this business?'

Doran shook her head.

'All right. You'll let us know, of course, if anyone should get in touch with you? If they've planted these pictures on you for a purpose you're sure to hear from them.'

'Unless,' Rodney offered, 'it's all a clumsy attempt to discredit my wife. Tempting her to sell something valuable under false pretences.'

'Can you think of anyone likely to do that, sir?'

'Well, no. Just a thought.'

'How could I sell them?' Doran asked. 'Without a provenance for them, and an explanation of where they'd been all these years? If they're real, there'd be a vast amount of money involved.'

'How much?'

'I can't say. A Rossetti painting made well over a million a few years ago. Another one fetched a hundred and eighty-five thousand. These aren't paintings, but any Rossetti, especially of a known sitter, would be into tens of thousands, and there are twenty-seven of these.'

'So we're talking internationally, are we? Overseas interest in them?'

'Absolutely. The Japanese in particular. They haven't any blonde women of their own, you see, and they immensely admire the Pre-Raphaelites' ones, especially Rossetti's.'

Claybourne shared a genuine smile with his sergeant.

'And they'd be eager to shell out for them. But only with authentication?'

'Certainly.'

A few more questions, then they were free to go. The package of treasures was left behind.

'Incredible, how guilty one can feel,' Rodney said as they emerged into the refreshing sea air and returned to the car. 'Think what you could have got into if you'd held on to those drawings. A perfectly nice chap, Claybourne, I'm sure, but a little of him goes a long way.'

'He was helpful,' Doran agreed. 'Will you drop me off at the shop and go on home?'

Something about the offhand way she said it troubled

him. He had fastened his seatbelt with an automatic action, but he suddenly unclasped it again and turned to face her.

'All right. But listen, darling – and I'm serious. I want you to give me your word that you'll try to put all this Rossetti stuff behind you. I've said this before, but now I'm saying it once more and for all. Something very dangerous has been around you, ever since this started. I know it fascinates you – it does me, in a way – but for your sake, and mine, and Kit's, will you promise to drop it now?'

'Yes, of course. It's done me no good, I know. Only, someone's going to get in touch with me about the drawings. They're sure to, whatever's behind it all.'

'Stall them off, and call me – or Claybourne. No more trying to deal with it by yourself. Understand? Anyway, it hasn't happened. If it does, we'll deal with it then.'

He clicked the belt back into place and started the car.

He set Doran down at the end of the pedestrianized street where the shop was.

'Be good. See you at home. 'Bye.'

She waved as he drove off.

FAIRWEATHER ANTIQUES was no longer a welcoming prospect in the small side street, off the main pedestrianized area. She thought how downmarket it looked. Only fit for the fate it was doomed to, once she left it. The window was overdue for cleaning. Behind the glass a Newlyn-type picture stood on a miniature easel. A good copy of an Art Nouveau dancing girl figure swirled her draperies at a pleasant but unremarkable crystal decanter.

Inside, Doran realized how little there was to tempt any serious buyer. All but the worst of her pictures had gone, snapped up by impressionable treasure-seekers, looking for valuable art in disguise. It had brought her a small rush of income, but it hadn't occurred to her to take advantage of her recent publicity by raising the prices. That was one of the ways she missed Howell – he would have told her to.

The huddle of furniture was much reduced, revealing even more obviously that the boy-with-dolphin garden statue which remained had lost several vital and prominent parts of his anatomy, and that they had been less than perfectly replaced.

Doran sighed. The familiar workplace seemed suddenly stuffy, lonely, even faintly hostile, as though it were rejecting her, knowing that she was forced to reject it. She felt an urge to seek out company: one of the other local dealers, or even the woman at the new boutique who never stopped talking about her problems. It would be nice to go and show off one's new hairstyle before it had a chance to lose its freshness. But that would mean all the bother of locking up again and resetting the alarm.

She wandered into the back room, missing the presence and personality of the longcase clock, now taken by Howell to sell for her in London. It had been a rewarding job to do, and an amiable companion.

Which reminded her of Ancilla. Why hadn't she thought of contacting her before, to pour the story of the drawings into her sympathetic, ready ear? She had reached for the telephone and dialled, before she remembered her promise to Rodney. But telling the tale to Ancilla didn't constitute a breach. She wasn't about to start a new line of investigation.

Anyway, it was unlikely that a busy person like Ancilla would be at home in the daytime. Her dealing activities had sounded strictly spare-time ones. In fact, there was no answer to her call.

For the rest of the morning Doran occupied herself with small repair jobs, mending some broken china and a pretty mirror frame. Then it was lunchtime. The Port Arms was comfortably warm on this chilly day, and there were cheese sandwiches and innocuous bottled cider.

Meg Rye, now raised from the doldrums by the excitement of flat-hunting further inland, came up and embraced her.

'Kiss, kiss. You're looking smashing today, Doran. Going out? Not your birthday, is it? Oh no, that would make you an Aquarian. Quite wrong.'

All the dealers were into astrology: it had its significance in decorative work. Doran agreed with Meg that she was anything but an Aquarian type, given to good causes and unable to care for less than two thousand people at a time. They chatted on about the stars, then changed to the ironical picking up of Meg's business with the first sunshine, the iniquities of the Council, and the increasing oddness of the pub's customers.

It was only chance that led Doran back to the shop by way of the public library. That, and the thought that they might have a new book she'd ordered for shop-reading. It was there. She collected it, then looked idly round for anything else. She gravitated to the reference section, and, almost automatically, to the art books – great, tempting volumes full of colour plates, many of them more recently published than those she and Rodney had at home.

Association of ideas lured her to the art biographies, more portable and just as tempting as the bigger tomes. A newish life of Dante Gabriel Rossetti almost beckoned to her.

She had given her promise; but just reading for interest wasn't the same as getting mixed up in anything. Without giving herself time to think further, Doran borrowed it.

Sitting in her shop's only comfortable chair, that inactive afternoon, she skimmed the story she already knew so well: Gabriel's upbringing in London, his pious mother and sister, his ambivalent view of women, the coming of beautiful Lizzie into his life . . . The rest was too familiar and sad to re-read now.

She skipped to the pages dealing with Rossetti's stay at Herne, where she and Rodney had gone looking for traces of him – how long ago? It seemed like light years, but was only three months or so. She read on. In that same summer of 1878, said the author, Dante Gabriel had suffered a shock, when, walking in a London Street, he had found himself looking at a shop-window display of a set of drawings by himself.

But not by himself – forgeries. For a moment he had been deceived, then saw them for what they were, clever copies, and some inventions, in his style.

Worse – they carried 'sold' labels. The embarrassed artist was forced to make enquiries and find the deceived buyer, and write to the *Athenaeum*, warning that there might be more circulating.

So, who had been the forger? Doran half expected it to say Hollyer, with his photographic process. She was only informed that the forger had never been traced, but that strong suspicion pointed towards one Charles Augustus Howell. She smiled at the echo of her former partner's name. Coincidence was at its mocking worst again. This earlier Howell had been, it seemed, a sort of wheeler-dealer in art circles, a slightly dodgy character. Something more in common with her Howell than just a name: she must pull his leg about it when she saw him next.

Charles Augustus's real name had been something else, apparently – he had claimed to be a Portuguese nobleman. He'd been useful to Rossetti and others as go-between, retailer of news, agent, and general dogsbody. Venal, someone had termed him: of dubious honesty, an amusing teller of tall stories, an unscrupulous self-seeker. Doran read with increased interest that it had been he who had organized Lizzle Siddal's exhumation, and the return of the manuscript poems to Dante Gabriel – in return for 'the swellest drawing conceivable' of his wife. In fact, the whole exhumation idea had been his.

And, the passage concluded, he had been a brilliant forger, with considerable help from his talented mistress, Rosa Corder.

Doran raised her eyes from the page. Could this chance discovery explain the astonishing, too-perfect, perhaps-not-quite-right drawings? Even so, it still gave no clue to the reason for their arrival in her hands. If only she'd kept them a little longer – been able to go through them again, with this new information.

But a promise was a promise. She put down the book and went to examine the mirror frame she'd worked on before lunch. It had stayed glued. Mechanically, she began to clean its plump Viennese cherubs, pink roses and true-love knots, glancing from time to time at her reflected face, imagining the ghostly features of Charles Augustus Howell behind it. Leering and winking, no doubt. He would be dark-complexioned if he was Portuguese. Dark-haired, almost certainly bearded. She was startled to find herself visualizing him in the likeness of Ralph Janner.

The telephone shrilled, making her jump. She put the mirror down too abruptly, so that it shed a newly-fixed corner.

The voice at the other end was all too familiar. She had heard it last at the Mill House.

CHAPTER TWELVE

'So you're there,' Janner sounded pleased with himself. 'I thought it'd be easier to talk without that domestic gaggle of yours taking your attention off me.'

'Hardly a gaggle. And I wasn't aware that you'd been introduced to them.' Doran knew with absolute certainty that she must talk for the sake of talking, and stay as calm as her jumping heart would let her.

'Never mind that. You've got the drawings?'

Careful. Don't give away a thing until he's shown his hand.

'Yes.'

'Beautiful, aren't they?'

'Very.'

'And genuine Rossettis.'

'They seem so.'

'Good, good! So far our friend Hollyer hasn't made a cynic of you for life?'

'I hope not.' Doran perched on the edge of a chair and took a deep breath, as he went on.

'You must have thought it a funny way of getting them to you – the luggage locker.'

'I did, rather.'

'Yes. Well, I didn't want to hand them over personally this time. The police seem interested in me, for some reason.'

'Do they?'

'Too interested. Someone's been talking – I hope it's not you, Doran – so I've had to move on. Again. Just as well I travel light. Which is why I don't want those Rossettis finding their way back to me. Understand? You're going to sell them for me, aren't you? And that's a statement, not a request. You – are – going – to – sell – them – for – me.'

Doran heard herself saying. 'I have sold them.'

A stunned silence at the other end. Then, 'Already? I don't believe it.'

'Already. I had a buyer, you see – a cash buyer for top Pre-Raphaelite stuff. I simply rang him, and he came down and picked them up.'

'And – paid for them?'

'Yes.'

Janner gulped. 'How much?'

'Just over half a million,' she replied simply. Emboldened by her lies she was becoming inventive. 'There were two he didn't like and absolutely refused to take, but I expect I can flog them somewhere else. I know it was very impulsive and probably very wrong of me to sell the things without knowing the owner, but I couldn't resist a firm offer, and cash. What dealer could?'

'Well, well.' Janner's tone was admiring. 'And I thought you were a high-principled sort of bitch. But you're all tarred with the same brush, aren't you? However, just as well for you that you managed to ditch your squeamishness. I'd have had to put some pressure on you otherwise.'

'How unpleasant that sounds,' Doran said politely. 'By the way, why did you give me the Rossettis to handle? Me, rather than someone big – a West End dealer, say?'

A hesitation. 'I'd heard about you. That you had good taste.'

'You've met me twice.'

'Before that. I heard that other dealers trusted you.

I even thought you could get away with selling the Hollyertype.'

'Thanks. And lose my reputation, when someone found out what it was?'

'Listen.' He was impatient now. 'I want that money. What have you done with it – where is it now? Because I want it.'

Doran, thinking furiously, tried to sound convincingly vague.

'I've got it at home, while I waited to decide what to do. It's all right, nobody knows about it. Nobody's going to find it. I'm glad you've got in touch so soon, though. How shall I . . . ?'

'You're going to bring it to me.' She had the impression that he had turned away from the telephone, covering the mouthpiece. It gave her time to wonder what sort of trap she was going to be led into. To meet him anywhere would be to confront danger – murder, even, when he found she had no money for him. If he wasn't quite up to murder, had he an accomplice who was?

'Where?' she asked sharply into the silence. What was he doing? Consulting a map, preparing his snare for her?

He was back. 'London, tonight.'

'I can't. Not possibly.'

'Why?'

'There isn't time. I've got a family – remember? My domestic gaggle. A husband and a little boy. I can't just not go home to them.'

'You won't have a home at all for long, if you don't do as I tell you.'

Panic was rising in her. Rodney wouldn't let her go to meet him. She knew she wouldn't be able to convince him she was going for any other reason. Besides, she had promised him, no more involvement. But if she failed to turn up the police would lose their best chance of catching him.

Desperate, she said, 'Listen, it's too difficult to come to town, and I'm too afraid, having to carry all that cash. Come to Barminster, or Eastgate – or Abbotsbourne. You know Abbotsbourne, don't you?'

She was sure he did. The person who had left Ophelia in the river and dumped Janey on the tomb certainly knew it. Her suspicion was confirmed by a touch of amusement in his tone.

'You like to dictate your own terms, I gather. All right. Name your rendezvous, then.'

The Lady's Last Throw. What was that? Something about a glove being flung into a den of lions? Rodney would know.

'How about,' she tried hard to sound cool, 'the church-yard? The tomb where the Jane Morris body was left,' she risked adding.

It sounded ridiculous. He would never buy it. But he did.

'You share my sense of the macabre, it seems. Not frightened of ghosts then?'

'I do happen to be a clergyman's wife.'

'So you are. Not the usual sort, though. Well, you're putting me to a lot of inconvenience, but no doubt you've got your mind set on your commission – if you haven't taken it out already.'

'I haven't.' That at least was true. 'And I need it.'

He sounded reassured. 'Right. Nine o'clock, then.' Abruptly he hung up.

Doran slumped back in her chair. Her knees were shaking and her mouth was ash-dry. She felt as though she had just crossed a four-lane motorway swarming with traffic.

He would see through her suggestion, of course; would know that she would never keep such a rendezvous alone. Most likely, on thinking it over, he would wonder whether she had the money at all. She ought simply to have told him she had handed the drawings to the police. There was nothing he could have done but expend his frustrated rage in a verbal attack.

She must have been mad to expect him to believe she had sold the drawings so quickly. But, he would think, she would scarcely agree to meet him if she hadn't. So, if he came to Abbotsbourne, it meant that he believed her.

Someone had remarked that there was a suggestion of simple-mindedness about that curious device of using the locker as a post box. The corpses' costumes had been oddly childish, as well as nasty. So had his attempt to drug her – not to mention his own silly use of disguises, almost a kind of child's game. Such a man might be deceived after all. At least, one could pray he might.

Besides, to make nothing of the opportunity would leave the pathetic girl and boy unavenged; and how many more victims, perhaps? If there was the slightest chance that Janner had been taken in, and would come, she must be there to meet him.

She locked up, and walked rapidly to the police station.

Inspector Claybourne was off duty. She was shown in instead to see Detective Inspector Grimwade, whose name she had heard Sam use as an old mate. As the conversation got under way Doran sensed that here was the man who had passed on to Sam the off-the-record information about the two murders. Good, so he was already primed about the case: just as well, in view of the fantastic new story she had to tell.

Grimwade listened with growing surprise. After his long years in the force he was surprised by very little, but this came as an exception.

'You were taking a big risk, telling him you'd sold them,' he said. 'Even bigger, offering to meet him.'

'I had to. I want him caught.'

'So do we. You do realize, though, there's nothing solid to link him with the murders? Still, possession of hard drugs is another thing; and yes, we would like to get a feel of his collar, as they say. I can't help wishing you'd picked a better place.'

'There wasn't time to think. Why not the churchyard? No-one much goes there.'

'Somewhere crowded would have been better. A pub, a restaurant. Where plain-clothes men hanging about wouldn't be noticeable. It won't be exactly easy tucking them away behind gravestones. They're big fellows, you know,' he added with a reassuring smile.

'I'm sorry. I hadn't thought of that.'

'Never mind. It's our problem, and we'll sort it out somehow. We'll be there, though you won't see us. You keep your mind on yourself, young lady. This type sounds a bit of a Mad Hatter to me. Another thing – if he flogs heroin you can be pretty sure he's on it himself – or something else. So watch yourself. We don't want another corpse on a gravestone.'

Doran promised. There was something else she needed to ask him.

'Have you – have they found out who the two victims were?'

He riffled through the file that Doran had seen before. It was visibly thicker now.

'The girl – traced by a photograph – in Liverpool. Bridie Donellan, age eighteen. Father a farm worker. Ran away from home last year, thought to have made for

London. Never wrote. Family don't seem to have tried hard to find her.'

'And the boy?'

'Not identified. Doctors said he'd been living rough a long time. Age about twenty.'

' "A youth, to fortune and to fame unknown",' murmured Doran. 'I was right about that. So what will they put on his tombstone?'

'Now, how should I know that, Mrs Chelmarsh?'

'They could call him Thomas Gray.'

Grimwade smiled again, humouring her this time. 'Why Thomas Gray?'

'It's a nice name. And appropriate.'

The walls of Bell House seemed to close round Doran that night, warm and protective, urging her to stay within them and be safe. Vi had spent one of her polishing days, beeswaxing the old wood of tables to a mellow shine, highlighting the few pieces of silver which stood on them. The fire was burning particularly well, lending semblance of life to little porcelain figures, giving the portrait of a Georgian gentleman a mysterious chiaroscuro.

From the kitchen wafted the alluring fragrance of a casserole into which Rodney had persuaded Vi to put some garlic. It was his favourite dish, and to accompany it he proposed a special wine from the few hoarded good ones in the cellar.

'But it isn't any special day, is it?' Doran asked, alarmed. She *had* to go out, and she needed all her wits about her. It would scarcely do to find herself stumbling over graves in a state of semi-intoxication.

'Every day is special,' Rodney pronounced. 'What about – no, St Valentine's past, and St Scholastica – pity. I'm rather fond of her. What would you say to St Felicitas and St Perpetua?'

'I don't know, not having been introduced. Rodney, about the wine – can we afford it? I mean, oughtn't we to save it for guests?'

He rambled on, oblivious to her protest.

'Two young mothers, mistress and maid. Carthage, second century. Condemned to the lions, but very fortunate to be beheaded instead. Their feast day's actually tomorrow.'

'Then I'm glad for them – about the lions, I mean – but I still don't feel we ought to have wine.'

Rodney was clearly disappointed. He enjoyed pleasures far more if they were shared with her. It would do her good, he said. She was looking peaky again. The night was cold, it would rain later, or perhaps frost would fall. It would be cosy with a fire and food and wine.

'We do have the odd half-bottle somewhere,' she said. 'You drink that.'

Kit was particularly loving when Doran put him to bed, holding on to her hand, playing the Walking in the Garden game up and down her arm. He insisted on telling her the Tale of Tom Kitten, instead of her telling it to him, which was entertaining and in some ways a slight improvement on Beatrix Potter, but took much longer. When she and Rodney finally sat down to dinner it was past eight.

He raised his glass. 'Uncompanionable – but I propose a toast. To the end of the Rossetti Connection.'

Doran touched her lips with Malvern water and murmured something inaudible. She was a traitor to Rodney. She had promised solemnly, and was about to break that promise in a way that endangered herself and possibly her family. 'You won't have a home for long if you don't do what I tell you,' Janner had said. What was he threatening? Fire? A bomb this time?

Then there was the police ambush. Would it work?

Suddenly all sorts of doubts attacked her. She had set herself a nightmare assignment. It would be madness to go to the meeting place. She was sorely tempted to tell Rodney everything. Rather than that, she decided suddenly, she would just not go. That was the answer.

Rodney enjoyed his meal, not noticing that she had given herself very little of it and didn't eat all of that. He had a second helping, called for cheese after the pudding, and, unusually, coffee. The clock hand was creeping very near to nine.

Doran abruptly pushed back her chair and stood up.

'Darling, you finish your wine with coffee. I must have some air. I've got to go out.'

'*Out?* On a cold night like this, after being in a warm room? You aren't feeling ill, are you? Darling?'

In that moment she almost did tell him, seeing the anxiety in his eyes, hearing his deep concern for her in his voice. But if she told him he would certainly stop her.

'No, I just need some air. I'm sorry. No, don't hold me.'

She was out of the room door, catching up her coat as she hurried through the hall, then out into the black night.

Because she knew the ground so well she could keep up a near-running pace, until the steep slope up to the Square forced her to slow down. The church clock was beginning to boom out nine as she reached the lych-gate. The few street lamps were behind her, the churchyard acres of darkness lightened only by the pale shapes of tombstones.

Nobody was in sight. Nobody appeared as she crept slowly along the side of the north transept wall, towards the Peacocke tomb. It was all so still. No policeman could be concealed and silent here. Something had gone wrong. They weren't coming.

No Janner, either. Perhaps he hadn't fallen for it. He had thought it over and seen through her impulsive lie. She felt the envelope stuffed with old papers that she had tucked in her deep pocket, to hand to him in order to play for time, as Claybourne had instructed her. What an infantile, melodramatic plan it all was. Not a plan, an impulse, which the police had gone along with to humour her.

Her hands were clammy-cold, her feet soaked from the wet grass. If only she had managed things better at home, had a better excuse ready for going out, changed into boots . . . It had all been so hasty. Rodney would be desperately worried.

The hum of an approaching car startled her into utter stillness. It would be Rodney, searching for her to make her go back. Or it *could* be Janner . . .

The car stopped, its door slammed. She heard the creak of the lych-gate and firm footsteps on the path, coming her way. They were getting closer, suddenly soundless on the grass.

Doran saw the approaching outline of a figure. It didn't seem tall enough for Janner.

The sudden upswing of a pocket torch blinded her. When it was lowered she found herself confronted by the radiant smile and glittering puffball halo of Ancilla Ireland.

Ancilla laughed.

'Expecting somebody, Doran?'

'I thought . . . I'd no idea . . . Yes, I was waiting for someone. Someone you don't know. How do you come to be here, Ancilla – you of all people?'

'Let's sit down, shall we? We must look like a couple of ghosts having a reunion. These Peacockes built good solid tombs for themselves, didn't they? Calm down, my dear.'

A warm gloved hand clasped Doran's icy one, as they sat on the tomb's flat top.

'You see, I felt that I was the proper person to handle this, rather than Ralph. He gets so easily excited, and one can never quite count on what he'll do – such as going off with the money and forgetting our share-out. You wouldn't want that for me, would you, Doran?'

Doran's nightmare was becoming more and more fantastic.

'Money?'

'Yes, all that lovely money. You know, I didn't quite believe it – that you'd sold the goods so quickly. But then I remembered how much you needed your commission, and when you fixed on this extraordinary rendezvous – well, I knew that it all hung together. You really are a very good dealer, my dear, and so transparently honest. That's why I chose you to handle the drawings.'

'*You* chose me . . . !'

'I had to have some backing from the trade, you see, with anything in the least – well, not quite kosher.'

'And the drawings aren't? And you knew?'

Ancilla spread her hands. 'Yes, but who's to say, other than a Rossetti expert? And I take it their new owner isn't one?'

Doran was able to answer more calmly. 'You could say that.'

Ancilla went on, 'Only a rich enthusiast would pay up so eagerly. And, of course, I did know where they came from.' She shivered suddenly. 'What a horribly uncomfortable place this is to talk in. Why don't we go into the church?'

'It's kept locked. Where *did* the drawings come from, Ancilla?'

'Birchington. When Rossetti was dying there he gave them to a servant or nurse or whatever, because she admired them. But he did put a note in with them saying "Not by me". They got passed down from hand to hand, and of course the note vanished somewhere in the process. Ralph heard of them through one of his contacts, and we got hold of them. After a bit of difficulty,' she added reflectively.

'You mean you took them – by force?'

Ancilla shrugged. 'Old people can be very awkward. And we didn't know she had a bad heart. I told you, Ralph does tend to get over-excited.'

Keep her talking, Doran thought.

'Who *is* Ralph, Ancilla? Why do you work with him, if he's – unreliable?'

'My dear, Ralph is a nutter. A frustrated artist – wanted to be a great painter, found he couldn't even draw well, could only daub. Went peculiar and started dressing up in Victorian artists' styles, hoping some of the genius would rub off on him, perhaps. Pathetic, but one humours him, he's so useful.'

'Do you . . . are you – lovers?'

'Good God no! But you might say we're loners. Both of us. And both mad about money. Not just petty cash – loads and tons of money. Buying and selling for our Eastern suppliers, you know. Lucrative enough, but we both wanted an art sideline, so – well, that's why you and I are here.'

'But with all the antiques trade to choose from, why pick on me?'

Ancilla laughed kindly. 'Ralph spotted that piece by Rodney in his Local Lore, or whatever it's called, and then your gay Welsh friend told me at the party about your fixation with Lizzie Rossetti. I thought at once, the perfect agent for our pre-publicity campaign – gullible, romantic, some knowledge but not too much, rather hard up . . .'

'Publicity for what?'

'For the Birchington drawings. We'd already got them, and we wanted to work up the market's interest in Rossetti.'

'I should have thought there was plenty.'

'Not for fakes, my dear – if that's what they'd turned out to be. We didn't dare get them looked at by an expert, you understand. We simply wanted them handled by a genuine enthusiast, who would believe in them enough to convince a gullible customer.'

'So you cultivated me.'

'I picked you up, my dear, and, well, insinuated myself into your affections. Applied charisma, you know? Psychological courtship. Making people believe they're tremendously important to one, flattering them stupid, never taking your eyes off them, listening to them instead of talking – there's no limit to the power you can get over them.'

'I thought charisma meant charm.'

'Haven't I that?' Ancilla under-lit her own face with the torch, smiling.

'Oh yes. You have that, Ancilla.'

'*Thank* you.'

'But it was all lies. You didn't like me – us?'

'Not a bit. But don't feel depressed about it. I don't like anybody. Only animals. I adore them, I worship them.'

'Tybalt?'

'Lovely, darling Tybalt. Of course.'

Doran was trying to keep her thoughts straight. Where *were* the police, then? Waiting for a man to show up – or just late? She had to keep the conversation going.

'So you planted that Hollyertype on me, as bait. Did you also kill those two kids?'

'No,' Ancilla replied matter of factly. 'Ralph did. He

213

quite enjoys it. He likes getting people into hard drugs and then doing things to them. I pass on that. I believe he tried it on you. But don't worry about these two – they were nothing, nobody, junkies off the street without a future. Ralph had a lot of fun dressing them up . . . Now, I think I'll have the money, if you don't mind. It's getting extremely cold.'

Doran's hand closed on the envelope in her pocket. But for the two of them the churchyard was deserted. She could try making a run for it, but Ancilla was fit and strong and in full command of herself, which Doran was not. But it seemed her only chance.

She took out the envelope and handed it to Ancilla, who switched on her torch again to examine the contents. While she was occupied, Doran backed gingerly away into the darkness, getting the tomb between herself and Ancilla. Then she ran.

She dashed between graves, over them, dodging tall stones and low surrounds. She knew the ground well by daylight. She had often walked there with Rodney after his Commination service:

'Cursed are the unmerciful. Go, ye cursed'
into the fire everlasting which is prepared for the
devil and all his angels . . .'

This particular devil's angel was coming after her now, surprisingly clumsy-footed, shouting at her to stop, swearing in German. How odd, German . . .

The lapse in concentration cost Doran a stumble over a child's small stone. She went headlong. Instantly, Ancilla was on her, gasping and cursing as they rolled on the soaking rough grass.

Firm hands grasped Doran and pulled her away. She heard Ancilla swear again, this time in English, as she too was seized.

'Now, ladies,' Doran heard Claybourne's voice, 'shall we talk this over sensibly?'

She heard Sam Eastry, asking, 'Are you all right, Doran?'

Jack Grimwade said nothing. He was too occupied in restraining the struggling Ancilla.

CHAPTER THIRTEEN

Rodney said all he had to say about Doran's broken promise, and he pitched it fairly strong.

The shock of seeing a police car stop at the gate of Bell House was the climax of a dreadful evening for him. At one point he had decided to call in someone from the Kinchens to baby-sit Kit, while he went in search of Doran; then realized that he hadn't the faintest idea where to go looking for her.

The anticlimax of seeing her get out of the police vehicle, still shaking but unharmed, was overwhelming. Neither of them would remember much of what was said when they were alone together and the door bolted and chained: only that Doran kept repeating, 'I *had* to do it – please understand.'

In mid-morning Sam arrived, looking weary and much more than his age.

'Just wanted to see you're all right.'

'I'm all right,' she said. 'Shocked, that's all. Rodney tried to make me stay in bed, but I feel better going about as usual. But you, Sam – you look terrible. Do sit down.'

'Thanks. I wouldn't mind a cup of coffee, Doran.'

As she made it she asked questions. Rodney was out for a few minutes.

'What happened after you got her, Sam? Where is she now?'

'In the cells at Eastgate. They're taking her up to town this morning. Funny thing about that lady – fought like a tiger at first, then suddenly calmed down and started being quite nice to Jack and the others. Apologized for giving trouble, said she was afraid she'd hurt someone's eye. Never known a prisoner behave like that.'

'Applied charisma again,' said Rodney, who had come in. 'It's worked before for her, so she thinks it might work again.'

'Like getting her sentence reduced?' Sam said. 'She ought to get the maximum, that one. They've found a king's ransom of the stuff in her flat, too. Street value millions, they reckon.'

'How do you know?' Doran asked.

'Well – they went up there from Eastgate, soon as they'd got her nicked. And I asked if I could go, just for the ride.'

'You? But . . .'

'Yes, I know. Lydia isn't best pleased with me.'

'What was it like, then?' Doran asked eagerly.

Sam told them. A mansion flat in a new block, with walls big enough to take the tapestries that were Ancilla's specialities. Furniture out of the stately home glossy magazines, pictures by artists Sam couldn't name, but he thought they included Gainsborough. Three fat silver-grey pedigree cats flashing their golden eyes and lashing their plumey tails at the intruders, and yowling for food.

And, quite dead in a baroque bed, Ralph Janner, dressed in an old-fashioned costume that Sam failed to recognize, but which looked Victorian. A hypodermic syringe had fallen from his hand. Claybourne had examined his neck very carefully. Then they'd gone drug-hunting in the handsome ornate bureaux and tallboys, with their many drawers and compartments, some intricately concealed.

One way and another, Sam concluded, it had been an interesting and unusual night – even though Lydia wasn't pleased.

Doran said, 'Ancilla told me she only had a poky flat, and a strict landlord, and as soon as she could afford to she was going to move somewhere better and keep cats. She wanted to keep cats – and all the time . . . !'

'A good liar,' Rodney said. 'You believed every word. So did I.'

'By the way,' Sam remembered, 'all her papers were in the name of Ann Ireland. Nothing about her being called Ancilla.'

Rodney shook his head sadly at Doran.

'But Ancilla would appeal to you much more than Ann, darling. Pure Rossetti, and with overtones of holiness. A clever woman, that.'

'I don't think I shall ever believe anyone again,' she said. 'Except you two. But Sam, where did you and the others come from last night? I could have sworn there was nobody hiding in the churchyard.'

He grinned tiredly. 'Nor there was. Jack Grimwade had the sense to ring me when Claybourne told him you were going to meet Janner. It struck him that I might know the layout of Abbotsbourne churchyard better than anyone else. Quite right, of course, I know it like the back of my hand.'

'Not exactly supplied with ideal hideouts for cowboys and Indians,' Rodney remarked.

'No. But something else is – the Watching Chamber.'

'The Watching Chamber? – Ah!'

They knew exactly how clever Sam had been, in his capacity as special adviser. The chamber was high up at the side of the church's north wall, not as old as the main building, but built on at about the time of the Regency; when decent people were getting agitated by grave-robbers, sneaking back by night immediately after a funeral, to steal the corpse and sell it to a doctor needing anatomical specimens.

'Burke and Hare,' Doran said.

So it had been. Some churches built on extensions at a point giving a good wide view for the watchmen who sat up all night, ready to pounce on anyone coming into the churchyard carrying a spade. The need to keep watch ceased when surgeons were enabled to get anatomical specimens legally. In many cases the watching chambers were pulled down, but St Crispin's remained.

'Only used for lumber,' said Sam, 'but enough space for the six of us – after they'd persuaded Rev Dutton to give us the key. Oh, *and* they'd bugged the Peacocke tomb as well, so we heard everything you and your friend were saying.'

'My "friend",' Doran said bitterly. 'Brilliant work, though, Sam. Don't you think you ought to go home and get to bed now?'

Sam said uncomfortably, 'It's all I want, Doran. Only, if there's another cup of coffee I think I'll just wait till Lydia's gone off to school – it's one of her dinner days.'

When Sam had gone at last, Rodney conducted Doran to the little room in the house that she used for repair work and storage. He picked up a small canvas that was standing on the floor, its face to the wall. It was the portrait she had found in the saleroom.

He arranged it on a chair, right way round.

'Now,' he told her, 'that may or may not be Lizzie Siddal. Agreed?'

'Yes.'

'But you're not. You're Doran Chelmarsh, my wife and Kit's mother. Agreed?'

'Yes.'

Rodney removed the painting and sat on the chair himself. He drew Doran down on his knee.

'My darling,' he said gently, 'you got yourself in all

220

this murky business because you identified yourself with Lizzie. Didn't you? Even to growing your hair and dyeing it her colour. Because she'd lost her baby, and used to sit rocking an empty cradle. Because you'd never talk about your own lost baby. *Ours*. Isn't that it?'

'Yes,' Doran said. 'But I didn't realize.'

Tears were welling in her eyes and sliding down her cheeks. Rodney went on.

'So when we found the dead girl in the river your pity for her got mixed up with your pity for Lizzie – and for yourself. And so it turned into an obsession that led you to risk your life. Right again?'

'Right.' She was weeping, her face against his shoulder.

'And all this, really, because you were worried about our income, and lonely at the shop; without Howell.'

She sniffed damply. 'I suppose so. Hanky, please. You are clever.'

'Am I? But am I wise, or conscientious, I ask myself. If I had been I should have accepted that Wykeworth living, with all its challenges and unpleasantnesses. "Oft in danger, oft in woe, Onward, Christian, onward go", so to speak. But I didn't, and my weakness was very unfairly rewarded by the restoration of the family fortunes. There's a moral in that somewhere, but I think I won't chase it. Because it's all over now, and things are going to be all right again.'

'I do love you,' Doran said. 'Whatever the moral is.'

The family fortunes had indeed been restored, and to heights they had never reached before. It was Howell who sensibly worked out that the drawings belonged to nobody, officially: the work of a long-dead forger, stolen from an old lady at Birchington, now dead and with no heirs or estate traceable by the police. Janner had been their last 'owner', and was dead, too, with no record left of what, if anything, he had paid for them. Ancilla was denying any connection with the transaction.

So, Howell said, if the drawings belonged to anyone, it was to Doran. A lawyer agreed, and the police didn't seem to want to know. Howell undertook to sell them for her, and did – for an impressive price to a Japanese buyer who fell instantly in love with them, and was uninterested in their authenticity, disinclined, indeed, to believe that they were not genuine.

He maintained his oriental calm, unlike Doran, on the discovery by Sacheverell Isaac's oldest consultant, himself a Victorian but still with superb eyesight, that one of them *was* genuine. The old gentleman detected in the least attractive of them all, one of Fanny Cornforth, the unmistakable *DGR* monogram, lurking minutely in a detail of embroidery on Fanny's jewelled scarf.

'The date right, the style right,' he had reported. 'Unusually positioned, but Dante Gabriel was more than a little dotty by that time. There are other things – small signs of the Rossetti hand that no forger could have produced, and I'll stake my meals for the rest of my life on that. Can a man pronounce more seriously than that, even at ninety-odd?'

His authentication sent the portrait up to an astronomic price, which the Japanese paid with smiling acceptance. So one of the beautiful blonde ladies in his possession had actually been a close friend of Rossetti: the fact made it a pleasure to him to pay more for her.

'There you are, *merch*,' Howell said, slapping the cheque down on the Chelmarsh kitchen table. 'Told you I'd see you right. Told you to give up that tacky shop and live your life proper.'

'So you did, Howell. And thanks. For everything. Have a beer.'

He surveyed her with pride as she got it for him from

the fridge. She was pink-cheeked again, her brown curls shining: a credit to him, he felt.

Kit came running in, eager-eyed.

'Mummy, mummy! Paul's father's hound bitch has had her litter and one's a runt, he says, so he doesn't want it. Oh, can I have it, please, if I promise to look after it? Oh, please!'

Doran gave a mock sigh.

'That's all I need, a foxhound pup. Well, if Daddy says yes, all right. Now don't choke me, run along and find him.'

She turned to Howell. He had ignored the glass she had given him and was drinking in his disgusting habit from the can.

'It's getting crowded round here,' she said. 'He'll have another playmate, come the summer, too.'

'Let me guess. A moggy – some lousy stray nobody wants, seeing that Tibbles of yours has shoved off next door.'

Doran's cheeks turned a deeper pink.

'No. I had a scan at the clinic. Kit's due for a sister.'

'There, now! Didn't I tell you? Acting funny, you was.' Howell raised his glass.

'*Iechyd da, merch.*'

THE END

A SELECTED LIST OF CRIME NOVELS
AVAILABLE FROM CORGI BOOKS

☐	12792 2	THE COMPLETE STEEL	Catherine Aird	£2.50
☐	13579 8	AT DEATH'S DOOR	Robert Barnard	£2.99
☐	13645 X	A CITY OF STRANGERS	Robert Barnard	£2.99
☐	13237 3	BODIES	Robert Barnard	£2.50
☐	13368 X	CORPSE IN A GILDED CAGE	Robert Barnard	£2.99
☐	13365 5	DEATH AND THE PRINCESS	Robert Barnard	£2.99
☐	13480 5	DEATH IN PURPLE PROSE	Robert Barnard	£2.99
☐	13651 4	DEATH OF A SALESPERSON	Robert Barnard	£2.99
☐	13129 6	THE DISPOSAL OF THE LIVING	Robert Barnard	£2.50
☐	13127 X	OUT OF THE BLACKOUT	Robert Barnard	£2.50
☐	13364 7	MOTHER'S BOYS	Robert Barnard	£2.50
☐	13128 8	POLITICAL SUICIDE	Robert Barnard	£2.50
☐	13479 1	SKELETON IN THE GRASS	Robert Barnard	£2.99
☐	13412 0	THE BANDERSNATCH	Mollie Hardwick	£2.99
☐	13236 5	PARSON'S PLEASURE	Mollie Hardwick	£2.99
☐	13664 6	PERISH IN JULY	Mollie Hardwick	£2.99
☐	13411 2	UNEASEFUL DEATH	Mollie Hardwick	£2.99
☐	13292 6	THE QUEEN'S HEAD	Edward Marston	£2.99
☐	13293 4	THE MERRY DEVILS	Edward Marston	£2.99
☐	13294 2	THE TRIP TO JERUSALEM	Edward Marston	£2.99
☐	13350 7	THE GETAWAY	Jim Thompson	£2.99
☐	13351 5	THE GRIFTERS	Jim Thompson	£2.99
☐	13241 1	KING BLOOD	Jim Thompson	£2.99
☐	13257 8	WILD TOWN	Jim Thompson	£2.99
☐	13239 X	THE KILL OFF	Jim Thompson	£2.99
☐	13258 6	THE RIP OFF	Jim Thompson	£2.99
☐	13736 7	PAST RECKONING	June Thomson	£2.99
☐	13497 X	ROSEMARY FOR REMEMBRANCE	June Thomson	£2.99
☐	13591 7	THE SPOILS OF TIME	June Thomson	£2.99